the
billionaire's
Secret Love

The Winters Saga

Book 2

IVY LAYNE

GINGER QUILL PRESS, LLC

The Billionaire's Secret Love

Copyright © 2016 by Ivy Layne

All rights reserved.

This book is a work of fiction. Names, characters, places, and incidents either are products of the author's imagination or are used fictitiously. Any resemblance to actual persons, living or dead, events, or locales is entirely coincidental.

Find out more about the author and upcoming books online at www. ivylayne.com

CONTENTS

CHAPTER ONE
TATE

*G*o out to dinner with me.

No, thank you.

The conversation echoed in my head. *No, thank you?* Had she really turned me down? I couldn't remember the last time a woman had turned me down. For anything. My first reaction was to ignore her and pretend I didn't care.

I couldn't do it.

I had no idea what it was about this girl that had so captured my attention. I'd only met her an hour ago, but I wanted her. I'd gone over to her apartment, geared up to confront her roommate over dumping my cousin, when Emily had opened the door and I'd tumbled head over heels after one look. It was the oldest cliché and one I'd never believed. Until now.

Taken part by part, she wasn't anything special. She shouldn't have been. Medium height, a little on the tall side but not quite tall. Long, straight, dark brown hair. Creamy skin. Gray eyes. And very, very curvy. Her faded jeans fit her sweet, full ass to perfection, and her sweater hung loose off one shoulder, clinging to her round tits. Her clothes hadn't been chosen to show off her body, but they were too well cut to hide it.

Still, it was her eyes that got me. A clear, pure gray, like a lake in winter. She'd swung the door open, and I'd fallen into those fathomless gray eyes. If I was being honest, I still hadn't pulled myself out.

No, thank you.

I couldn't stop hearing her refusal, repeating on a loop in my brain. Why had she said no?

I'd figure it out. First, I had to help my cousin, Holden, and Emily's roommate, Josephine. Who would have guessed I'd be playing matchmaker? Or really, fairy godmother. Godfather. Whatever. I was the last guy to believe in relationships, but there was something about the way Holden talked about Josephine. She wasn't just a hook-up to him, and when it had looked like she was blowing him off, I'd stepped in to save the day. Now, all I had to do was get Jo a bag of ice for her hand and get out of the lovebirds' way. That was fine by me. I had my own potential hook-up to worry about.

I left Emily standing outside the office door in Mana, the night club Holden and I owned, and ducked behind the bar for the ice. Jo had punched the guy who tried to break them up, and her knuckles were bleeding. As soon as I took care of her, I could focus on dealing with Emily, who was standing outside the office door, her back pressed to the wall, arms wrapped protectively around her middle.

I was pretty sure she'd never been in Mana before. She didn't look like the type. Maybe that was why I found her so appealing. I was used to women in short skirts with perfectly styled hair and too much makeup. Emily didn't look like she'd done more than pull a brush through her thick, shiny hair all day. She definitely wasn't wearing makeup. On her, it didn't matter. Unadorned, Emily was more beautiful than any woman I'd seen in recent memory.

Hoping I was interrupting something, I unlocked the door to the office to find Holden standing in front of Josephine, cradling her injured hand in his. Looked like they'd already figured things out. Just in case, I said to Jo,

"You good?"

She didn't get a chance to answer. Holden did it for her. "She's good. You can go."

"*Are* you good?" Emily asked from behind me. Jo promised that she was, and Emily stepped back to leave the lovers in peace.

I heard the lock click on the office door and grinned. Nothing like the feeling of a job well done. If I hadn't gone to confront Josephine, they never would have realized the loser on her team was keeping them apart. I didn't normally interfere in Holden's love life, but I'd never seen him so messed up over a woman. If for no other reason, I'd wanted to get a closer look at the woman who'd broken Holden's heart.

She wasn't my type, but I could see why Holden was crazy about her. Josephine was pretty, with a lush body and a sharp brain. A lot like Emily, except Emily was more. She was luminous, beautiful in a quiet way that seemed to have hooked my heart and mind along with my dick. And finally, we were alone.

Turning to her, I said, "Do you want me to show you around?"

She shook her head, eyes searching for the door. Damn. I'd been hoping the club would be a way in, but it looked like Emily was more interested in leaving. Mana was the hottest club in town, almost impossible to get into, and I was offering her free run of the place. I hadn't expected her to say no.

I was proud of Mana. It had started as a hobby. A friend of mine had gotten in over his head and needed to sell out. Holden and I had the money to buy the club, and we thought it would be a good time. We'd tossed around the idea of opening a club for years, mostly for fun, never thinking we'd actually do it. We had our hands full with WGC, our gaming company, and neither of us needed another project. But we'd happened to have a chunk of liquid cash from an investment that had just paid off at the same time a good friend, who was also a club manager, had been looking for work. We hadn't been able to turn down the opportunity. Between the three of us, Mana had become one of the places to be seen in Atlanta, and we were all making a ridiculous amount of money from it.

Emily was edging her way back down the hall toward the door to the alley. I shook my head. The girl was a mystery. Most people would kill to get into Mana, and she was trying to escape. I should have been annoyed. I was not known for my interest in difficult women. Easy was my motto.

I know what you're thinking, but cut me some slack. I'm not entirely an asshole. You have to understand, I'm a Winters. In Atlanta, that means power, wealth, and influence. It doesn't hurt that we're all reasonably intelligent and good looking. The kind of women that pursue wealthy men *because* they're wealthy generally don't care that much if they're not attractive, but it's a bonus. Who wouldn't rather catch a rich, hot, young guy than to have to marry some old geezer to get the good life? I was used to living with a target on my back.

Both Holden and I had spent our lives fending off the

women we didn't want and helping ourselves to those we did. I never led them on, never implied that I was interested in anything more than a good time. And, yeah, I wasn't used to women turning me down when I asked them out. It probably makes me a sick bastard that Emily's refusal only made me want her more.

I had the feeling if I didn't take charge, Emily was going to sneak through the door, into the alley, and out of my life. Fortunately for me, it looked like her best friend and roommate was now with my cousin, so even if she ran, I knew how to find her. But I wasn't letting her get away tonight without trying again. Reminding myself that I was charming and good with women, I followed her down the hall and caught her at the door, just as she was easing it open, checking furtively over her shoulder to see if I was following.

Gotcha.

"I can get home from here," she said.

"I know. Do you want me to drive, or would you rather walk?" I asked, deliberately misunderstanding her. Her apartment wasn't far, maybe a fifteen-minute walk, but if she thought I was letting her go on her own, she was crazy. The neighborhood was fairly safe, and it wasn't late, but I'd see her home. I wasn't always a gentleman, but I like to believe that if my mother had lived past my fifth birthday, she would have raised me to have good manners.

"I'll walk," Emily said, turning to the end of the alley. It was clear she intended to do so without me. Tough luck.

"It's a nice night for a walk," I said agreeably, falling into step beside her.

"Are you sure you don't want to go out to dinner with me?" I asked, keeping my tone light and unthreatening. I didn't want to browbeat her into a date, but I had to figure

5

this girl out, and the only way to do that was to keep her talking. Since she didn't seem inclined to get the conversation rolling, it was up to me.

"I'm sure," she said in the same prim tone she'd used when she turned me down the first time.

I looked at her, asking myself why I was so determined to win her over. At the sight of her long, dark hair shining in the streetlights, and her determined stride that did nothing to hide the sexy sway of her ass, I remembered. I wanted her. I wanted to peel off that T-shirt and take her prim tone with it. I wanted those clear gray eyes to go dark with lust while I fucked her senseless. I needed her to want me back.

Curious, I took her elbow in a loose grip as we crossed the street. Not wanting to scare her, I let go almost immediately, but not until I felt the shiver that went through her body at my touch. Her eyes flicked at me for a second, and I saw what I needed to know. She wasn't afraid of me, and she wasn't indifferent. She felt it too.

"So, just out of curiosity, why won't you go out with me?" I asked.

She risked a sidelong glance at me before her eyes skittered away. "I don't date."

"You don't date? At all? Are you into women?"

She raised a delicately arched eyebrow at me.

"It's a viable question," I said.

"Your assumption is that I must not like men if I don't like you?" she asked, her formerly prim in tone now frosty, arms crossed tightly over her chest.

I shrugged. "I'm just trying to figure you out. If you're not into women, are you saying you don't date anyone? Ever?"

"I don't have time for a social life," she said. "I have a

dual concentration, and I'm working for two professors this semester."

"Everyone has time for some kind of social life," I said, knowing it was true. She was busy, but so was I, and I still managed to get out of the office.

"I don't," she said.

I took her arm as we crossed another street, enjoying the way she trembled at my touch. I wasn't going to give up.

"Then it's not me you don't like," I said. "It's dating in general."

"I haven't been on many dates," she admitted. "But they've always been a waste of time."

"That's because you haven't gone out with me."

She laughed. My ego might have suffered from her laughter, but the sound was unexpectedly beautiful, her cool voice transforming into something as clear and crisp and gorgeous as her gray eyes. I wanted to make this girl laugh again, to feel that sound falling over me, the joy and delight suffusing her, chasing off her restraint. I wished I'd been looking at her eyes when she laughed. I had a feeling they would be as alluring when she was amused as I knew they would be when she was aroused.

"There's nothing I can say to change your mind?" I asked. She shook her head. Maybe it was my self-confidence talking, but I thought she looked a little regretful.

"I'm sorry," she said, actually sounding like she was sorry. "I know this is difficult for you, since it seems no one ever tells you no, but I really do have to decline. I don't have time to date, and I'm not interested in being your flavor of the week."

"Hey, it's not like that," I protested, even though, with other women, it was exactly like that. Emily came to an abrupt halt on the sidewalk and turned to face me, her eyes narrowed.

"It's not? You're looking for a girlfriend?"

I shifted my weight and fought the urge to squirm under her assessing gray gaze. Normally, people only saw what I wanted them to see—Tate Winters, the youngest male in the Winters clan, successful businessman and killer with the ladies. I liked to keep things on the surface outside my family. I'd learned the hard way that when I let people in, they were usually only interested in digging for scandal or money. Emily seemed to see more. Her eyes studied me, and somehow, I knew she knew that the Tate Winters everyone else saw was a front.

When I didn't answer, she said, "I thought so. Look, you seem like a nice guy, and it was very cool of you to come over and straighten out the whole mess between Holden and Jo. But I'm not going to sleep with you, and I don't have time for a relationship, even if you were interested in one, which you're not. Going to dinner with you would be a bad investment of my time."

She turned back toward her apartment and started walking again, leaving me behind. I caught up and walked beside her in silence, running various arguments through my mind and rejecting them. I thought about offering to sleep with her outside a relationship—that was an efficient use of her limited free time—but I got the feeling that casual sex was not on her agenda. Offering it would probably not improve my case.

That left me in a unique situation. Sometimes, when a woman said she wasn't going to sleep with me, she was playing a game. I didn't know Emily well enough to say this with certainty, but I was pretty sure she meant exactly what she'd said. She had no intention of sleeping with me. We were both working under the assumption that I didn't want a girlfriend. Was I sure about that? I'd never wanted one before.

I walked beside Emily in silence, sneaking glances down at her, watching the way the light played over her gleaming hair, how her hips swayed with every step, her round tits jiggling just enough to tease my imagination.

I didn't know if I wanted a girlfriend. I did know I wanted to pry this woman open and find out what was beneath her cool composure. I needed to know everything, inside and out—what she was thinking, what she looked like naked, how to make her laugh, how to make her come.

We reached her building, and I walked her up. I left her at her door, saying only, "It's been a pleasure meeting you, Emily."

I was tempted to try to kiss her goodbye, but I held back and was rewarded by a flash of confused disappointment in her striking eyes when I left without pushing for more.

She had one thing right, I thought as I walked back to the club. If all I wanted from her was a fuck, then I was wasting her time. What she didn't know was that if I decided I wanted more, she didn't stand a chance.

CHAPTER TWO
EMILY

I closed the door to the apartment I shared with Jo and flipped the deadbolt, listening as Tate's footsteps echoed down the hall. I leaned my forehead against the wood and drew in a deep, slow breath, trying to slow my pounding heart. The entire night had been way out of my comfort zone. At first, I'd been carried along by emotion. Tate had showed up to confront Jo when he thought she'd dumped Holden, and since Jo had spent the last few days crying over Holden dumping *her*, I'd been furious at the sight of him.

Then, once we'd figured out what had really been going on, we'd all been pissed with Jo's teammate, Darren, and had gone off to confront him. Distracted by the drama, my anxiety had been pushed into the background—right up until Tate had asked me out to dinner. For a split second, my heart had leapt in my chest with a flare of excitement and joy. Tate was hot—gorgeous like I'd only seen in movies and magazines, with deep blue eyes, thick, dark hair, full, kissable lips, and an athletic build that said he knew how to use his body. Yum.

He was also very smart. The gaming company he ran with Holden had developed one of my favorite games, and the industry was rife with rumors over their new, top secret, projects. Hot and smart. I had no plans to fall for any guy, but if I did, it would be a man exactly like Tate. A second after he'd asked me out, my breath had frozen in my lungs, and the joy in my heart had turned to terror. I couldn't go out with Tate. I couldn't go out with anyone, but I definitely couldn't go out with Tate. Prickles ran down my arms, my nerves firing off as fear mounted in my chest. I'd tried to force myself to breathe, to fight off the ringing in my ears. It was a losing battle. It had been a while since I'd had a panic attack, but sitting in his car with my emotions out of control and his blue eyes demanding an answer, I'd felt one threatening. I'd forced myself to breathe and said, "No, thank you."

No, thank you?

I'd heard my own voice as if from the end of a long tunnel. *No, thank you.* Was that what I'd said? I was such a ridiculous dork. I wasn't surprised that he looked shocked. For one thing, I doubt any woman had ever turned him down for a date. And second, who said *No, thank you* when someone asked them out? Apparently, I did. I didn't have a lot of practice. I couldn't remember the last time anyone had asked me out.

A part of me wanted to go to dinner with Tate. Wanted to go desperately. The part of me that had a killer wardrobe, even though I never went anywhere but home and school. The part of me that still dreamed of more than professional success. That still believed in fairy tales.

The part of me that wished I were a different girl. In the last few years, I'd managed to get the worst of my anxiety under control. I'd had to figure out how to handle it if I wanted to pursue my Masters degree at Georgia Tech. If I ever wanted anything resembling a real life. I couldn't do that if I never left my parents' house. With determination and a lot of hard work, I'd done it. I was a year and a half into my Masters program, and in all that time, I'd only had one anxiety attack. It hadn't even been a bad one.

I reminded myself that compared to my life a few years before, I was already living my dream. I'd come so far from the reclusive shut-in I'd been in high school and college. But I hadn't come far enough to get tangled up with Tate Winters. He was so far out of my league, it wasn't funny. I was a 23-year-old computer science geek, a virgin who had never been on a proper date. Tate had slept his way through the most beautiful women in Atlanta. He was gorgeous, successful, wealthy, and notorious. Even if I thought he was interested in me—not just for sex, but in getting to know me —I could never handle the attention that came with the Winters family.

I'd been doing well in the last 18 months, but a lot of that was due to careful planning. If I avoided crowded places, got to lectures before the room filled up, and talked to people I already knew, I was mostly fine. I'd had severe anxiety, combined with agoraphobia, since I'd been a kid. Since the shooting. I'd walked away undamaged on the outside. What had gone wrong inside my head took years to fully develop, and once it had, I'd become a prisoner of fear.

Medication had never helped much, but I'd found a therapist while I was doing my undergrad online, living at home, who helped me find ways to manage out in the real world. I was getting better. Sharing an apartment with Jo instead of living at home was a major accomplishment. Ditto for attending my graduate programs in person.

But I wasn't anywhere close to taking on a boyfriend,

much less equipped to deal with a man like Tate. I'd done the right thing by turning him down. I knew I had. If I'd taken him up on his invitation to dinner, I would only have been a disappointment. I wasn't beautiful or sophisticated, and I had no experience with men. When I got up the nerve to try a relationship, I'd start with someone I knew—maybe one of the guys from school.

A little voice in the back of my head piped up to remind me that none of those guys had ever made me shiver with a simple touch. At the memory of Tate's strong hand on my arm as we crossed the street, I shivered again, my nipples tightening, an ache rising between my legs. He was out of my league, and the idea of going out with him was impossible, but Tate Winters was the most beautiful man I'd ever seen. Every time I thought about him, I wanted what I couldn't have.

Straightening, I tried to think about anything other than Tate. At least I was alone. Jo had been all cuddled up to Holden when I'd left Mana. I was pretty sure she wasn't coming home anytime soon. I loved Jo. She was the ideal roommate and my best friend. Even so, after the drama of the evening, it was a relief to be alone. Deciding to take advantage of my solitude with a bath, I put on a soundscape that I used to ease tension and turned the taps on hot. Our apartment wasn't luxurious by any means, but the tub was a little bigger than average. Perfect for me. I loved taking baths.

Anxiety was a bizarre condition, I mused as I poured lavender scented bubble bath under the streaming water. Most people were afraid when they were alone. Jo had confessed that when she'd first moved to the city from her small Midwestern town, she'd been freaked out to be alone in the apartment. I was the opposite. I felt the safest on my own. It was people that cranked my anxiety levels into the panic zone. Being in the club earlier, I'd thought I was going to lose it. A night on my own and a relaxing soak would go a long way toward calming me down. After a good night's sleep, I might even be back to normal.

I climbed in the tub and lay back, letting the hot water soothe my tight shoulders. I tried to think about school, but the vision of Tate's blue eyes invaded my mind. I couldn't believe he'd asked me out. Remembering the look on his face when I'd turned him down, I laughed. Poor Tate. He clearly wasn't used to hearing the word *no*.

My amusement died as I thought about how much I'd wanted to say yes. It wasn't just that he was hot. And I didn't care about his money or who he was. Actually, I would've liked him more if he'd just been a normal guy.

I'd grown up in Atlanta, and I knew who Tate Winters was. His parents had died a few years after the shooting that had sidetracked my life, and I had vivid memories of watching the Winters children subjected to a media hell storm in the wake of losing their parents. I knew from bitter experience what that was like. Being stalked, the flash of lights, the shouted questions. The way the reporters would pop up out of nowhere and refuse to leave you alone. A part of me thought that it wasn't so much the shooting that had messed me up, but everything that had come after. Watching Tate, his brothers, and his cousins suffer the same terrifying attention, my heart had hurt.

So I knew who he was. I knew there was a lot more to him than just the good-looking playboy splashed across the *Style* section of the paper. His company, WGC—Winters Gaming Corp.—had made two amazing games, and there were rumors they were developing a new type of physics engine and had made advances in emerging gaming that would turn the industry on its ear. Yeah, there was a lot more to Tate Winters than what he showed on the outside.

It was foolish to wish that I could have the brain and the body without everything else that came along with being a Winters. He was who he was, and that was his whole package. But I wished I could have said yes. I let my brain slide into a fantasy where I did say yes. A fantasy where Tate took me out and we talked all night, and then he took me home.

I wasn't a complete innocent. Well, I was. I'd barely been kissed. Embarrassing, I know. I was 23 years old, and I should have been on my second or third boyfriend by now, at least. I just . . . I was always so busy trying to pretend I was normal, trying to manage the anxiety, that I never had the chance to actually *be* normal. Boys were one stress too many. I'd been mostly okay in the few years after I survived the shooting, gradually becoming more and more shy, then fearful, but it hadn't seemed dangerously out of the ordinary at first. I'd never been very outgoing and always remained on the quiet side, like my parents, so none of us noticed that by the time I was 13, I rarely wanted to leave the house, even to go to school.

By the time I should've been going on my first date, my agoraphobia had gotten so bad that I was being home-schooled, isolated from my peers, with boys the last thing on my mind. It took years of trying, changing therapies and changing doctors, before we hit on an approach that really worked. I'd hated every second of it, but in the end, I was here at Georgia Tech, doing a dual concentration in the computer sciences department focused on graphics and intelligent design in gaming. People spent years trying to get into this program. Not only was I here, but I was living in an apartment and not with my parents.

I was doing it. I was living life, a great life, a successful life. I was going to finish my program and get an amazing job. My dreams were going to come true. I just didn't think I had room in them for a guy, much less a guy like Tate. My life was a perfectly calibrated balancing act, and Tate Winters was a wrecking ball.

I thought about that fantasy of a date, about what would happen after he brought me home. Would I want him to go slow? To seduce me? Despite the hot water, my nipples tightened. My legs fell apart, one knee knocking against the side of the tub, and I was grateful once again to be alone in the apartment. I slipped my hand between my legs and stroked one fingertip over my clit, thinking about Tate.

He wouldn't have to work hard to seduce me if we ever got that far. Just the thought of him, and I was wet. I raised one hand to cup my breast, squeezing my sensitive nipple between my fingertips, imagining my hands were Tate's. He'd had big hands, not a surprise since he had to be a few inches over 6 feet, with broad shoulders and a strong build. His hands—the memory of how they felt holding my arm as we crossed the street—made me shiver.

I wanted to feel those hands on me, just once. I swirled my finger around my swollen clit, then dipped it inside, pressing the heel of my palm down on my clit. I was tight, not a shock, since my fingers were the only thing that had ever been inside me, and at the thought of Tate touching me like this, my muscles clamped down even tighter. I might not ever have gotten this far with an actual man, but I was no stranger to the pleasure my body could bring me. I was inexperienced, not a prude.

Too aroused to fight it anymore, I let my head loll back and pushed another finger inside me, grinding my palm down hard, imagining I was with Tate and those weren't my fingers—it was his cock fucking me, pounding inside me, filling me up, making me come. I cried out his name on a gasp as the orgasm washed through me.

I'd needed that. It had been a while since I've made myself come, and usually, an orgasm like that would hold me for a while. I squeezed my legs together in the cooling bathwater and realized, now that I had Tate on my brain, my own hands weren't going to be enough.

CHAPTER THREE
TATE

Proving that I had good manners, I knocked on Holden's door before I let myself in. That, and I knew he probably had company. I liked Josephine, but I didn't think Holden would appreciate my seeing her naked. I waited at least a minute, maybe two, before knocking again, this time a little harder. Holden hadn't come into work all day. It was late afternoon. They couldn't still be having sex. Eventually, he answered, his mismatched sweatpants and torn T-shirt suggesting that maybe they had in fact still been having sex. Or at least, they had still been in bed.

I wasn't going to let that stop me. I was on a mission.

"What are you doing here?" Holden asked as I walked through the open door and into his kitchen.

"Sorry to interrupt," I said. "But I need to talk to Jo."

Holden shook his head. "No way. Jo's busy."

"Do you think you can let her out of bed for five minutes?" I asked. Heading for the fridge, I said, "I can get myself a beer and wait."

"Tate, you're my favorite cousin, but if you don't get the hell out of my apartment, I'm going to kill you."

Fortunately, as I straightened from the open fridge with a beer in my hand, I heard footsteps at the end of the hall. I just needed a few minutes with Holden's girl, and then I could get out of their hair.

Josephine walked up to Holden and tucked herself into his side as she said, "Hey, Tate. Did Em get home okay last night?"

"That's what I wanted to talk to you about," I said. Her forehead wrinkled in concern.

"Is she okay? Did anything happen?" Jo asked, worry weighing down her voice.

"She got home safely. I walked her right to the door," I reassured her.

"So, what's up?"

"I want her number," I said.

"Did you ask her for it?" Jo raised her eyebrows as if she already knew the answer.

"No," I admitted. She made it sound so easy, but after the way Emily had shut me down, I'd been fairly certain she wouldn't give me her number. "I asked her out, and she said no."

"Sorry," Jo said, sounding like she meant it. "Emily doesn't date."

"I'd like to change her mind about that," I said, trying to look sincere and trustworthy. Josephine shook her head.

"I can't," she said. "I can't give you her number. I'd have to ask her first, and if you thought she wanted you to have her number, you would've asked her yourself, right?"

She had me there. But I wasn't going to give up that easily. Meeting Josephine's blue eyes with my own, I said, "You owe me one, and you know it. If it hadn't been for me, you and lover boy over there never would've reconnected, and that douche in your program would've split you up with the virus he put on your phone. Do me a favor and just give me Emily's number. I promise I won't do anything to hurt her."

Josephine shifted against Holden, pulling away from him to cross her arms over her chest. She studied me for a long moment before she said, "Why do you want her number?"

"I want to take her out. I want to get to know her better." Her searching gaze dug beneath my explanation, demanding more. "I like her," I said. "I think there could be something there, but we'll never know unless we spend some time together." I turned away from Josephine and Holden to find a bottle opener in the drawer.

Holden let out a sigh. "Give me one of those," he said, nodding toward my beer.

"Josephine?"

"Sure."

I pulled two more beers out of the fridge and opened all three, sliding theirs across the white marble-topped island.

"So, you *like her* like her? Holden asked.

I thought about glaring at him, but instead, I said, "You're one to talk."

"Touché." His grin was completely unashamed. I wasn't sure what I was doing with my own love life, but I liked seeing Holden so happy. It almost made me feel bad about badgering his new girlfriend.

"The thing is," Jo said, interrupting us, "Em doesn't date. Anyone. Ever. And I'm not so sure you're the best guy for her to start with."

"What are you saying?" I asked. Josephine looked away and took a drink of her beer before answering.

"I'm not gonna tell you personal things about Emily. She's my best friend, and her life is private. But she's really shy. Off the charts shy. More than just shy. And you're not low-profile. I'm not sure you two would be a good fit."

"So I don't even get a shot?" I asked, starting to get annoyed. I just wanted to go out with the girl. I wasn't planning to kidnap her and ravage her against her will.

"It's just that," Jo went on, "Emily knows better than anyone what she can handle. She was definitely interested in you, and she's very interested in your work, so if she wouldn't go out with you, she had her reasons, and I don't feel comfortable going against that."

"What if I promise I won't call her?" I said, feeling the unfamiliar sensation of desperation rising in my chest. "I'll text her. I can be nonthreatening."

Josephine didn't respond, just stared down into the open mouth of her beer bottle, thinking.

Finally, she said, "I've never seen her react to anyone the way she did to you last night. Until she remembered to be nervous, she went head-to-head with you. Confrontation is not Emily's thing, but she was comfortable with you. And you have a lot in common."

Josephine fell silent again. I liked her with my cousin, liked the way they looked at each other. When Holden slipped his arm around her waist and pulled her tight against him, I liked it even more. The small spark of jealousy I felt only made me more determined to get Emily's number.

Emily had asked me if I wanted a girlfriend, and I hadn't answered. I didn't have a good vision of what having a girlfriend might mean. It was only in the last year or so that I'd started to think maybe there was more to life than sleeping with nameless girls, partying, and work. Watching

Holden cradle Josephine in his arms, knowing that once I was out of their way, he'd take her back to bed . . . yeah, I was jealous. I remembered the way Emily had yelled at me the night before when she thought Holden had dumped Jo, the way she'd pointed her finger at me like an angry school-teacher, her gray eyes sharp and filled with the passion of fury. I liked that girl as much as the quiet one who said, *No, Thank You* when I'd asked her out.

"I'll be careful with her," I said. "I promise. I don't know what I'm doing here, but I swear, I'm not looking to nail her and never call her again."

"You'd fucking better not be," Holden growled at me.

I rolled my eyes at him.

"Seriously? Would I be here talking about my feelings and begging your girl for Emily's number if I was just gonna sleep with her and ghost on her? Give me a little credit."

"'That's your usual MO," he said evenly.

"It's yours too," I shot back, "but look at you now."

"Okay," Jo cut in. "I'll give you her number. But, you have to promise to go slowly." Then, mysteriously, she said, "I don't think there are many people who will understand certain parts of your life as well as Emily. She's worth it."

I had no doubt Emily would be worth it. My gut was telling me that there were hidden depths to the girl, depths I would like. But I'd never find them unless I could get her to talk to me again.

I watched Josephine put Emily's number in my phone, her brow still furrowed in concern as she handed it back. I didn't stick around. I wanted to dig for more information on Emily, anything that would help me win her over, but I needed Josephine on my side, and I had a feeling if I pushed her too hard, her tentative approval would evaporate. It only took me a minute to go from Holden's place to mine, since our apartments split an entire floor of Winters House, the upscale historic retail/office/residential building owned by my cousin, Jacob. I shut the door behind me and flipped the lock out of habit, distracted by the phone in my hand.

I had the first step. I had Emily's number. Now I just had to think of what to say.

Figuring I might as well confess right off the bat, I typed out a text.

This is Tate. I badgered Jo for your number. Don't be mad at her. I was very charming.

I hit *Send* and waited, wondering if she'd answer. If she didn't, I'd have to think of something else. It took so long, I was about to give up when my phone chimed and I checked the screen.

I'd never be mad at Jo. But I doubt you were that charming.

I thought for a minute. She had to be teasing me. If she were really mad, she wouldn't have answered, right?

I was a little charming. I also refused to leave, and I think they wanted to get back to bed.

A minute later, she sent back,

So you were annoying. I can see that.

What are you doing right now? I typed.

Working on graphics for a game.

School or yours?

Mine, she answered.

What is it? I typed, curious.

I waited for a minute, then a link to the app store popped up with a note.

The sequel to this.

I clicked the link, which brought me to a game I knew. I'd played it when it had come out the year before. It was simple, but cool. Basically, it was an elaborate maze with

24

pitfalls and hidden treasure that you navigated by turning your phone. It was deceptive, because it looked easy, but as the maze advanced, it required finesse and patience. At the time, I'd thought the premise was unique, and the graphics were gorgeous, even in the small format of a phone screen.

This is yours? I played it. Amazing.

Thanks. I'm almost done with the next one.

You have to let me see it, I typed.

Maybe. I'll show you mine, if you show me yours.

Was she flirting with me? It was too much to hope for. I thought about making a suggestive comment to see what she'd say, but then I remembered Jo's warning. I'd just gotten Emily talking to me, or at least texting with me. I didn't need to scare her off. I typed,

Anytime.

There was a pause, then,

I have to get back to work. Later.

I'll try you tomorrow.

K.

I put my phone away, feeling both bereft and triumphant. The conversation had been short, but she wasn't angry that I had her number, she'd talked to me, and I'd learned something new about her. It was progress on all accounts. I couldn't wait to text her again. Tomorrow seemed very far away.

CHAPTER FOUR
EMILY

'll try you tomorrow.

K.

I stared down at my phone, my heart pounding in my chest. Texting should have been less nerve-racking than talking to Tate in person, but it wasn't. I wanted to be clever, maybe funny, but instead, I felt awkward. He'd said he'd try me tomorrow. My heart raced at the thought, this time not with nerves but anticipation. I closed my eyes, feeling the difference. Before Tate, every time my nervous system got excited, it was a bad thing. With him, it was different. This wasn't fear or panic. When was the last time I'd been excited like this? I didn't know. I could think of times I'd been excited about a project—the app I was working on or things we were doing in my program. I'd been excited when I'd gotten into Tech.

Excited by a person? Nope. And definitely not like this. I remembered touching myself in the tub, coming while I thought of Tate. No, I couldn't remember the last time I'd been excited by a person. I wasn't sure how to feel about it.

I was home alone again, working and eating leftovers.

Normally, I wouldn't feel the least bit pathetic about that. But with Jo at her new boyfriend's and the thrill of texting with Tate over, the rest of my evening stretched in front of me, feeling a little flat. Pushing the thought aside, I turned back to my computer and tried to focus on work. As I usually did, I got sucked into the game and ended up staying up half the night.

I was just getting out of bed the next morning when I heard the key in the lock. I hoped Josephine was alone, because I wasn't dressed for company, and I was barely awake. She was, and when she saw me, she looked sheepish and said, "Sorry."

"For what?" I asked, still half-asleep.

"Didn't he text you?" she asked, looking confused. "I was sure he'd text you right away."

In a flash, I remembered, and I knew why she'd apologized. "It's okay," I said, going to the coffeemaker. I needed caffeine.

"Then he did text you," she prompted, one eyebrow raised in question.

"He did," I said. "He admitted that he annoyed you until you gave him my number."

"I think he's a nice guy," Jo said. I shrugged. I wasn't sure what to think about Tate. "You're not mad at me?" she asked. I shook my head.

"Really," I said. "It's okay. He's probably going to get bored with me when I won't go out with him. There are a million other girls out there. He'll lose interest. It's not a big deal." There was a gnawing ache in my chest at the thought of Tate losing interest in me. No matter what I said to Jo, it felt like a big deal. It didn't matter. Tate Winters was not for me.

"I'm cooking dinner at Holden's house tonight," Jo said, hesitantly. "Will you come over?"

I thought about it. I liked Holden, liked the way he was with Jo. But I hadn't seen enough to be sure, and she was my best friend. I should go check him out. Suddenly suspicious, I asked, "Is Tate going to be there?"

"I didn't invite him, I swear," Jo said.

"Did Holden invite him?"

Jo shook her head. "We didn't talk about inviting anyone but you. I really don't think he did."

My knee-jerk reaction was to say no. *No, that's okay. I'll stay home and eat takeout.* I stopped myself before I could do it. It wasn't about Tate, not really. I wouldn't be surprised if he showed up. I knew he and Holden had the only two apartments on that floor of the building. To call them apartments was misleading—they were like mansions unto themselves. I'd only seen the first floor of Winters House—they had a killer coffee shop—but based on how big the first level was, the apartments above had to be huge. I got the impression from Jo that Tate and Holden were in and out of each other's places all the time, so if Holden was having company for dinner, it was likely that Tate would show up.

I wanted to see him again, and if he did show, it would be less stressful seeing him with Holden and Jo than it would be if I were on my own. That wasn't the only reason I thought I should say yes. The most dangerous part of my anxiety was the way it narrowed my life. It was always easier to say *no*, to stay home where I was safe. That was how I ended up home-schooled and agoraphobic when I was a teenager. The therapist who had helped me had taught me that facing my fear, learning that everyday life was not a minefield waiting to explode, was the only way to fix my problem.

It had been a grueling therapy. That first walk around the block by myself, I'd wept the entire time, shaking and sick to my stomach. When I'd reached the safety of home, I'd thrown up. The second had been a little better. I was still shaking and nauseous, but I hadn't puked. The third was one more step toward normal. It had taken me twenty-seven tries, but eventually, I'd been able to walk around our block with only the barest tingle of nerves. The same thing happened the first time I went to the grocery store by myself. Baby steps. And now that I was mostly functioning like a regular person, I had to be careful that I didn't start saying *no* too often. I was never going to be a social butterfly, and I'd always thrive with plenty of alone time, but there was no good reason I shouldn't have dinner with my friend and her new boyfriend.

"Okay, sure," I said.

Jo gave me a hug and whispered, "Thanks, Em."

* * *

I DRESSED CAREFULLY TO GO TO HOLDEN'S, JUST IN case. Being realistic, I knew I wouldn't see Tate. It was Saturday night, and he probably had plans that didn't involve his cousin. Still, I rarely went out looking like a slob. I'd started paying attention to my clothes as part of my therapy. A well-chosen outfit was my armor. Doesn't everyone feel better, stronger, when they know they look good? My face and body weren't anything spectacular. I ate more than I should and didn't get enough exercise, and my figure showed it, though my frame carried the extra weight well, and I was more curvy than lumpy. I had pretty hair, I thought, and great eyelashes. Thick, long, and dark, I never needed mascara. I liked makeup, though I rarely bothered with much of it. I preferred to put my time into my wardrobe. I didn't dress up too often. I didn't like drawing attention to myself, and surrounded by students in jeans and T-shirts, formalwear would have been too much. But everything I owned was deliberately chosen and fit me perfectly.

For dinner with Jo and Holden, I chose a pair of black leggings and a flowing black and cream striped tunic. It was casual and stylish without being showy, and it flattered my curves but didn't draw attention to them. I wasn't going to Jo's new boyfriend's house flashing cleavage. Jo, on the other hand, I dressed in my favorite push-up bra and a V-neck sweater. In her situation, flashing cleavage was completely appropriate. She wasn't that interested in clothes, and I always had fun dressing her up.

Holden greeted us at the door and took the bottle of wine I offered, saying to Jo, "I think I picked up everything on your list, but you might want to check."

A voice behind him said, "He never pays attention to his list at the grocery store."

Holden looked pained and shook his head. To me, he said, "Sorry. He found out you were coming over for dinner and refused to leave."

I looked past Holden to see Tate leaning against the center island in the kitchen, a bottle of beer in his hand, a grin on his face, and a slightly uncertain look in his blue eyes. I wasn't sure how I felt about seeing him again. His interest in me made me nervous for all sorts of reasons, some of which I understood and some I didn't want to examine. But I didn't want to make him feel weird about being in his cousin's house. I appreciated that Jo cared about my feelings and had obviously shared her concerns with Holden, but I didn't want to be an object of pity or curiosity. I'd come too far for that.

Hoping to diffuse their worry, I shrugged and said to Holden, "Don't worry about it. I'm cool."

Jo gave me a look, and I sent her a smile that hid my nerves. "Really, I'm fine. He's fine." Raising my voice a little so Tate could hear, I said, "He's like a big puppy. He doesn't take a hint well, but he's harmless."

Holden laughed when Tate said, "Ouch. I don't think I've ever been called a puppy before."

I shrugged. Ready to change the subject, I said to Jo, "Did you tell Holden about Darren?"

She shook her head.

"What about Darren?" Holden asked.

Darren was the guy who'd almost managed to keep Holden and Jo apart. A member of Jo's team for her HCI project, he had a crush on her and hadn't liked her blooming relationship with Holden, so he put a virus on her phone that blocked their calls to each other. They both assumed the other had lost interest, and if it hadn't been for Tate's interference, they would never have gotten together. He was a good guy, even if he was annoyingly persistent.

"So," Jo said, "You know I emailed Angie everything, including a copy of the virus I found on my phone."

"You said it had Darren's signatures all over it," Holden said.

"Everybody leaves signatures in their code. It's hard to avoid, but Darren's were so obvious. I even told him he should never make anything he didn't want traced back to him, or he should clean up his code, and he still made a virus. It's crazy how someone that smart can be so stupid."

"So tell him what happened," I urged.

"I am," Jo said to me. To Holden and Tate, she said,

"Angie—she's the head of my project—went through everything and even found that he'd been working on the virus at the lab."

She shook her head. I was right there with her. It was stupid enough that he made the virus in the first place—but hey, we all had our hobbies. To do it on one of the school's computers . . . I couldn't quite wrap my brain around how terribly foolish that was.

"What did she do to him?" Tate asked.

"She kicked him out of our project, for one. But then she passed everything along to the head of the department, and now he's under an academic review. He's probably going to get kicked out of school. I actually feel kind of bad." Holden wrapped his arm around her, pulling her tightly to his side.

"Jo, no," I said. "If he was willing to put a virus on your phone and ruin your relationship with Holden just because he was jealous, what else would he do? He clearly has no moral compass, and if you'd kept quiet, you'd just be leaving him free to screw with somebody else's life later down the road. And maybe that time, it wouldn't work out. Maybe that time, there wouldn't be a Tate to step in and fix it. Maybe it would be someone's job on the line, or worse. You had to say something. And you shouldn't feel bad about it."

"I know," she said, resting her head against Holden's chest. "I know. He's an enormous jerk, and I'm not sorry I punched him. And I guess I'm not sorry he might get kicked out of school. It's just that I know how hard we all worked to get in, and he'll never have a chance like this again. Plus, it makes me wonder what he'll do when he doesn't have anything left to lose."

"Don't worry about that," Holden said, his voice hard. I noticed his eyes meet Tate's, and I got the feeling they were having an entire conversation without words.

33

"We'll take care of that," Tate said. Jo let out a breath but didn't respond, seeming content to snuggle with Holden. I, on the other hand, wanted more of an explanation.

"What are you going to do?" I asked.

"We know people who can keep an eye on him," Tate said quietly, his blue eyes steady and serious.

"What kind of people?" My imagination was running wild.

"Have you heard of Sinclair Security?" Tate asked. I nodded. The name popped up in the news fairly often, usually in connection with high-profile clients like celebrities, politicians, and billionaires. "We grew up with them. The Sinclairs are like family, and on top of that, they handle all of our security work. Holden will let them know they need Darren on their radar. If he does anything even slightly sketchy, they'll have it covered."

Jo leaned back and looked up at Holden's face, wonder and concern tangling in her eyes. "Holden, you can't do that. They can't just watch him forever. It's too expensive."

"Nothing's too expensive if it keeps you safe," Holden said, lifting a hand to run his thumb along her jaw, his warm brown eyes on hers. "Sinclair Security has a long list of people they monitor. Adding one more is no big deal, and we have them on retainer. If there's an extra expense, I don't care. This guy is never going to bother you, or anyone else, again. Never."

"Okay, Holden," Jo said, her voice a little dreamy. Holden dropped his head to kiss her, and I looked away. I was happy for my best friend. No, not happy. I was thrilled, ecstatic, doing mental cartwheels every time I thought about her with Holden. But that kiss was getting a little too intimate. I remembered something she'd said about having sex on the kitchen island, and I involuntarily took a step back. When Tate's hand closed over my elbow, I jumped.

"Relax, it's just me," he said. Tugging gently, he pulled me out of the kitchen and into the spacious living room with windows overlooking the city and a huge couch facing an equally large television. "Your roommate's cute, but if Holden's going to fuck her in the kitchen again, I don't think I want to watch. I'd rather be alone with you."

At the look in his eyes, heated and intent, every muscle in my body tightened. Not in fear, but in anticipation. My head wasn't sure about Tate, but my body knew what it wanted—more of Tate.

CHAPTER FIVE
TATE

Emily hovered beside the couch, clearly trying to figure out a way to put some space between us. If she sat first, she knew I'd sit next to her. Her hesitance was endearing. I wasn't used to shy women. I'd never found shyness appealing before, but with Emily, I liked it. I made it easy on her and chose a spot right in the middle of the wraparound couch. As I guessed she would, Emily sat catty corner to me on the other side. Close enough to be polite, but not close enough to touch. Oh well. Touching could come later.

"Tell me about your game," I said, partly to relax her and partly because I genuinely wanted to know. It wasn't often that I found myself attracted to a woman who was not only a gamer, but a game designer. Tech as an industry tended to be a boy's club, and gaming was no exception. WGC made a point of hiring talented women, but the reality was that they were hard to find. Not enough females gravitated to the industry in the first place, and now that hiring women in tech had become a thing, it was even harder.

Plus, whenever I met a woman in my industry, my

instinct was to evaluate her as a potential hire. Not with Emily. I already knew, based on what she said she was studying, that she would be an ideal candidate for WGC. The company would have to do without her. I wanted Emily for myself.

Her natural reserve melted away beneath her enthusiasm as she explained the changes she had planned for the sequel to her game. When she said she had a demo of the first level on her phone, I put out my hand.

"Gimme," I said. Emily pulled her phone from her back pocket and stared at it for a moment. "Come on," I cajoled. "Just let me see the first level. Please? Pretty please?"

Reluctantly, she handed me the phone, the screen already open to the game. The design was familiar. I could already see she hadn't made any fundamental changes, but the graphics were deeper, richer, and more detailed. She leaned forward on the sofa, her eyes moving between the screen and my face. As I'd hoped, she wanted to see my reaction to her creation more than she needed to preserve the distance between us. After a few moments, she got up and sat beside me.

I don't know if it was perfume, her soap, or just Emily, but she smelled of the ocean, and something lightly floral. The heat of her leg pressing against mine and the fall of her silky dark hair against my arm were distracting. I forced myself to pay attention to the game, telling my cock to be patient. He would have his chance, I hoped, but not if he scared her off by getting hard the first time she sat next to me.

My cock didn't listen. I was glad I was wearing jeans and leaning forward, and doubly glad her attention was on the phone in my hands and not my lap.

I played my way through the first level, marveling at the

way she'd stepped up the sophistication of the game for the second version. When she apologized for the graphics, saying they were still a little rough, I shook my head.

"This is amazing," I said. "I wouldn't call it rough." I looked up to see her face only inches from mine, her gray eyes bright, her cheeks flushed. Her pulse thudded in her throat, and her pupils were dilated. It took everything I had not to kiss her. With any other woman, I would have had her flat on her back, her shirt halfway off. But with Emily, I knew I had to take it slow. Sometime before she left tonight, I was going to get my hands on her. Just not yet.

I eased back a little, giving her space, and turned my focus back to the game. The first level was a little more challenging than I would have expected, not that I had any trouble finishing it. I handed back her phone and said, "It's great. You have to let me play the rest when it's done."

"Thanks." At the sight of her cheeks flushed with pleasure, I stood, picking up our empty beers as I strode to the kitchen. I needed a little space before I did something I was going to regret. *Slow*, I reminded myself. *You're taking it slow.*

"Do you want another beer?" I asked over my shoulder.

Emily rose and followed me to the kitchen, saying, "Sure."

I was relieved to see that Holden and Jo were not having sex on the island, but at some point, they had stopped making out and were cooking dinner together. Good. Not only was I hungry, but I needed a distraction from Emily, from her sweet scent and her pink cheeks. From the full lips I needed to kiss. From every inch of that curvy, luscious body. When was the last time I wanted a woman this much and had only touched her elbow? I was completely out of my depth with Emily. Everything about her was complicated and difficult. I never stopped to ask myself if she'd be worth it. I already knew she was.

Dinner was good. Pasta with seafood, and Jo had made bruschetta that was delicious. I barely tasted it, more interested in watching Emily interact with the rest of us. She was initially quiet, but as she got comfortable with the rhythm of the conversation, she joined in. I was pretty sure she was enjoying herself. Jo and Holden were almost nauseatingly adorable, teasing each other, holding hands under the table, and generally acting like a couple newly in love.

Emily had a third beer with dinner, choosing not to try the wine she'd brought, saying that she had the taste of beer in her mouth and switching would be weird. I don't know why I found that cute, but I did. Jo got up to clear our plates, and Emily joined her. I caught her saying something about the bathroom and knew this was my chance. She hadn't had enough to drink to be drunk, or even tipsy, but she was relaxed and as comfortable as I'd ever seen her. If I was going to make a move, now was the time.

I was waiting for her at the end of the hall when she came out of the bathroom, just out of sight of Holden and Jo in the kitchen. Her face when she saw me waiting was priceless. Nerves, confusion, and excitement all swirled through her eyes, and I watched her trying to decide what to do. I didn't give her a choice, catching her by the arm and pulling her to me, turning her back to the wall. She was taller than average, but I was still bigger.

How to trap someone without making them feel trapped? That was the challenge. If I waited for Emily to come to me, I'd be an old man, still wanting her. It was in my nature to take charge, but I didn't need Jo's warning to know that if I was too aggressive, I was going to scare her off.

She looked up at me and said, "Tate?"

I didn't answer, not with words. Slowly, giving her plenty of time to push me away, I dropped my head. Triumph surged through me when, instead of ducking to the side, she raised her lips to mine.

I brushed my mouth across hers in a kiss so light it almost wasn't, before I went back a second time, lingering. Her eyes fluttered closed, and she let out a soft puff of breath. I skimmed my lips across her eyelids, her forehead, and each rounded cheekbone before they landed back on hers.

This time, I kissed her a little harder, opening her lips with my tongue. She gasped, her body melting into mine, and I wondered for a second if she'd ever been kissed before. There was something untouched about Emily. She was so unpracticed, every response genuine and unstudied. I dipped my tongue in her mouth again, rubbing it against hers, coaxing her open to me. Needing more, I wrapped one arm around her waist, pulling her to me, burying my fingers in her hair, and tilting her face to mine.

At the hesitant brush of her tongue, I thought I was going to lose it. It took everything I had to keep the kiss from spinning out of control. My cock was a steel bar. I wanted to pick her up and pin her to the wall, to grind myself against her and make her come through her jeans. I wanted to carry her out of Holden's place and across the hall to mine, to lay her across my bed and strip her naked and fuck her until she screamed.

I rubbed my tongue against hers, trying to keep my hands gentle. This was supposed to be a seduction. If I showed her what I really wanted, I would scare the hell out of her. Later. There would be time for that later as long as I didn't fuck it up now.

I had two choices—I could stop the kiss, or I could find a

way to dial it back before it spun out of control. I wasn't ready to end my first taste of Emily, so I dropped the arm I'd wrapped around her back and raised my hand to cup her chin, holding her face in my hands. My gut clenched when she raised her hands to my waist, keeping me where I was— not pulling me against her, but holding me close. If it was a victory, I'd take it.

I kissed her and kissed her, my mouth feasting on hers, tasting her, absorbing every breath, every whimper, every quiet moan, until we heard a voice say, "Emily?"

Then, "Jo, shut up."

"Holden." A giggle and what sounded like a smack.

I raised my head and stared down at Emily, feeling almost as dizzy and disoriented as she looked. Her eyes were wide, her pupils huge, her lips kiss-swollen and red. Pressing my advantage, I whispered, "Have dinner with me. Don't say no, Emily."

"Yes," she said in a dazed voice.

"Tomorrow."

"Okay, tomorrow," she agreed.

I went back for one more quick kiss before I said, "You won't regret it. I promise."

I hoped I was telling her the truth.

CHAPTER SIX
EMILY

At six o'clock Monday night, I opened the door of my apartment to see Tate leaning against the door frame, wearing jeans and an un-tucked blue button-down a few shades lighter than his eyes, his dark hair falling over his forehead. At the sight of him, my knees literally went weak. What was I doing? I didn't date. I've never had a boyfriend, and the night before had been my first real kiss. Now, I was going out to dinner with Tate Winters? It was insane.

Okay, I'd been kissed before. Hasty, fumbling attempts by boys as nervous as I was. Mostly, they were short, sloppy, and not repeated. Nothing like kissing Tate. That had been . . . I didn't have words. When I thought about that kiss, I saw starbursts of color and felt how hard my heart had pounded and the way my body had softened and melted into his. I wanted to be as close to him as I could, needing his hands on my skin.

He was going to expect more. I wasn't completely naïve, even though I was innocent, at least in terms of real-life experience. Men like Tate Winters did not go on platonic dates, and that kiss was a clear indication that platonic was not what he had in mind. To say I was nervous would be an understatement. I was terrified, though it was refreshing that, for the first time in memory, I wasn't afraid of having a panic attack. These nerves were different. I wasn't anxious. I was a brand new combination of anticipation, excitement, and the fear that I was going to make a total fool of myself.

It was too late to back out, not that I was going to. I opened my door to Tate, and he held out his hand for mine, saying, "Are you ready?"

I was not. I was not even remotely ready to go on a date with Tate Winters, but I wasn't going to admit it.

I grabbed my purse and keys off the table beside the door and took his hand. "I'm ready," I lied.

At least I looked good. In a role reversal, Jo had helped me get dressed. She correctly assumed that I was going to wimp out and wear something conservative. When I picked a pretty but demure cream-colored, cap-sleeved sweater, she'd snatched it out of my hands and handed me a hot pink, V-neck, slinky top with three-quarter sleeves and a high low hem. The shirt was made of a silk/modal blend that was soft and clingy.

It was way too sexy, especially when she handed me a push-up bra in the same hot pink. Why did I buy under-wear like this when no one ever saw it? Maybe because I secretly hoped that one day I'd be going on a date with a guy who would deserve sexy underwear. Now that the day was here, I was sorely tempted to dive under the covers of my bed and ignore it. If I tried to look too sexy, was I sending the wrong message?

I liked Tate. Understatement. I really liked Tate. He was smart. He was unbelievably attractive. Just kissing him had been better than my hottest fantasies of sex, and he

THE BILLIONAIRE'S SECRET LOVE

hadn't even touched me beneath my clothes. But I wasn't ready to have sex with him. I'd looked at the top and skirt Jo was holding and shook my head in indecision.

"Em, honey, you can't wear jeans and a T-shirt for your date. It's not you."

"That cream sweater is me," I protested.

"Not for a date, it's not," Jo said. "You bought this." She held up the pink top and the pink push-up bra in one hand, and the long, Navy, stretchy skirt in the other.

"I know . . ."

"Honey," she said gently, "you don't have to do anything you don't want to do. You just need to be yourself. And you know you don't want to wear job interview clothes on a date. You know you don't."

I took the clothes from Jo and put them on. She was right. She usually was. I didn't want to wear frumpy clothes to go out with Tate, and I wouldn't have said yes if I didn't trust him on some level.

So here I was, holding his hand and walking down the hallway of my apartment building, wondering what the hell I had gotten myself into. He seemed to know how nervous I was, because he kept up a steady stream of conversation, telling me about his day and asking me about mine, until I relaxed. At least, until we pulled up in front of his building.

"I thought we were going out to dinner," I said.

"We are," he said. "And no, I'm not taking you to my place. Not exactly."

He pulled his car into the parking garage behind the building, coming around to open my door after he'd stopped the car. He reached down and took my hand to help me out, then leaned down and pressed a kiss to my lips before stepping back and saying, "You look beautiful."

"Thanks, so do you," I said, then squeezed my eyes shut.

He did look beautiful, but you weren't supposed to call a man beautiful. I waited for him to laugh at me.

He said, "Thank you," without a hint of amusement in his voice. Something inside me relaxed just a little.

I followed him into the elevator, wondering where we were going. When we stopped on the fourth floor, the door slid open to reveal a lobby, the letters WGC on the wall.

"We're eating here?" I asked. "Really?"

"I said I'd show you around if you agreed to have dinner with me, and I always keep my promises."

"Really?" I asked again, speechless with excitement. "Are you going to show me what you've been working on?"

"Some of it," Tate said. "But you have to sign an NDA first. Not very romantic, sorry, but there's stuff I can't show you without it. Unless you don't want to see . . ."

"I figured I'd have to sign a nondisclosure if I could get you to show me anything. I'll sign, absolutely. I can keep my mouth shut."

Tate led me through the doors and into the silent office. The lights were dim or off in most of the workstations.

"There are usually a few people working after hours," he said. "But tonight, I told them all to get out and go home. If anyone shows up, they're fired."

I laughed. "You didn't."

Tate looked down at me, his blue eyes both amused and serious. "I did. I knew you wanted to see the company, and I didn't think you'd want a crowd. Besides, I want you all to myself."

He led me through the open part of the office, past conference rooms with glass walls and whiteboards, all the way to the back. Two offices with glass walls faced out, overlooking the rest of the company. These must be Holden and Tate's. One was dark. In the other, low lights illuminated a huge glass and metal desk facing six enormous monitors on which I could see a screensaver of WGC's flagship game, *Syndrome*. A wicker picnic basket sat in front of the monitors, oddly old-fashioned on the ultra-modern desk. The lid of the basket was half-open, the neck of a bottle of wine poking out. A picnic? He was going to show me their top-secret project, and he brought a picnic? He was good.

"What do you want to do first?" Tate asked. "Eat dinner, or take a look at what we've been working on?"

There was no contest. Rumors had been swirling through the gaming community for the last six months about WGC's top-secret new project. Consensus was that it had to do with the new physics engine, but nobody knew for sure, and WGC's employees were notoriously tightlipped about company business. I was dying to see what they were doing, and an empty stomach was no diversion.

"We can eat later," I said, practically vibrating with excitement. It said a lot about what a geek I was that, temporarily, I was more hyped up about seeing the secret project that I was about being so close to Tate.

Tate curved his hand around my shoulder, the heat of his skin burning through my thin silk top, and just like that, the butterflies in my stomach were all about Tate.

"Take a seat," he said. "I'll be right back."

I was just settling into the plush high-backed leather chair at his desk when he returned with a sheaf of papers in one hand, pushing another wheeled leather chair in front of him. He set the papers on the desk in front of me, along with a pen. I was glad I was a fast reader. Otherwise, I probably would have signed the nondisclosure agreement without looking at it. It was fairly standard, and this wasn't the first time I'd had to sign an NDA. The year before, I'd worked on a project that had required a high level of secrecy. I knew how to keep my mouth shut. I finished scanning the document, then signed and dated it with a flourish, almost bouncing in my seat in anticipation.

When Tate rolled his seat beside mine and leaned into me, sliding one arm around my shoulders, I thought the top of my head was going to blow off. My heart pounded and my body tuned in to Tate, my brain torn between interest in his project and its fascination with the man himself.

Tate took the mouse, woke up the computer, and opened a game simulator program. "This should give you an idea of what we've been working on," he said.

"Is this the sequel to *Syndrome?*" I asked. *Syndrome* had been a first-person shooter about the aftereffects of a viral infection in a post-apocalyptic version of the United States. Its combination of heart pounding action and intricate problem-solving had made it an instant hit. The graphics on the screen looked like those from the original game, but they were far more finely rendered. As the wind blew a piece of crumpled paper down the deserted street on the computer screen, I had a hard time convincing myself that what I saw was a game and not a video recording. Tate nudged the mouse in my direction, and I started to play, my eyes wide, captivated by the level of detail in the game environment as it reacted to my character. After a few minutes, I tore my eyes from the screen and looked at Tate.

"What kind of processor does it take to run this?" I asked. "There's so much going on, so many small details."

"It needs a little more than the current standard," Tate admitted, "but not as much as you'd think. We found a way to disguise the redundancies so it looks like everything around you is responding to your character, even the things you can't see, but underneath, there's less going on."

My brain raced to figure out how they had done it.

Unable to resist, I turned my attention back to the game and was quickly sucked in when a group of mutant zombies—the introductory enemy from the original game—attacked me. I wasn't ready for it, too distracted by the game environment to think about battle tactics, but I'd been gaming since I was a kid, and before I'd taken too many hits, I figured out the basic mechanics and was on my way to defeating the mutant zombies.

"Yes! That's right, bitches!" I shouted, rocking back in my chair as the last zombie fell to my roundhouse punch.

"Nice job," Tate said from beside me. I jolted upright, instantly flushing bright red. I was on my first date in a million years, with the most beautiful, sexy man I'd ever laid eyes on, and I'd just exposed what an enormous a geek I truly was. I was tempted to drop my head to the desk, but that would only have made it worse.

Tate must not have minded, because instead of laughing at me, he cupped my face in his hands and kissed me. At the touch of his lips, I completely forgot about the game, the physics engine . . . anything that wasn't Tate.

His mouth took mine with leashed possession, claiming me with his kiss but holding back. His hands stayed on my face, his lips and his tongue exploring my mouth, the only place he touched me, but my body responded as if we were naked, skin to skin.

My breasts swelled and my nipples tightened. I shifted in my seat as he shifted between my legs, my body ready for more even as my brain struggled to keep up.

I leaned into him, reaching for him, not sure what I planned to do with my hands but wanting to touch. Before I could figure it out, Tate broke the kiss, his fingers trailing along my jaw and down my neck.

I stared at him, mesmerized by the heat in his deep blue eyes. "Sorry," he said. "I couldn't help it. You were too cute."

I flushed and looked away, a little embarrassed and a lot giddy. Without thinking, I said, "We probably shouldn't play together then. We'd get distracted too easily."

"I'm good with getting distracted, if that's how we do it," Tate said.

"Me too," I whispered.

CHAPTER SEVEN
EMILY

"Do you want to eat dinner?" Tate asked. Checking the clock on the computer, I realized I'd been playing the game longer than I thought. It was a common hazard with gaming. You could login planning to play for only a few minutes, then find that hours had disappeared into the virtual world.

I wasn't sure what I wanted. I wanted to keep kissing Tate. I wanted to play more of the game. And my growling stomach piped up to remind me that I also wanted something to eat. More kissing was the clear winner, but I didn't think I was ready to handle where that was leading, so I said, "Dinner sounds good."

I helped Tate unpack the picnic basket. At my raised eyebrow when I saw he'd chosen the wine I bought when I wanted a splurge, he said, "I cheated and asked Jo." After the wine, he pulled out box after box of sushi, each one marked with the familiar logo of my favorite restaurant. I didn't have to look in the boxes to know they would be all my favorite rolls. So far, Tate was stacking up to be the perfect guy, thoughtful, patient, and an amazing kisser, not to mention crazy smart, and a game developer. If I tried to hand design Prince Charming, I wouldn't have done this well. As long as I could forget that he was also a Winters, and everything that went along with it, I might find myself really falling for him.

Who was I kidding? I was already half-gone, and this was just our first date. Now that we weren't kissing or gaming, my nerves cranked back up. Then Tate said, "How did you decide on Tech?"

I left out the parts about the shooting, my agoraphobia, and the fact that just getting to graduate school had been a miracle—forget about going anywhere out of state. Instead, I told him about how I'd wanted to go to Georgia Tech since I was a kid, which was also true. We fell into an unexpectedly easy conversation, skating over the big stuff like my anxiety and his family. I told him more about the game I was working on and how I'd been surprised when it had sold well enough to pay for a year of school with a little left over, and he filled me in on some of the advances in emergent gaming that they were putting in *Syndrome* 2, in addition to the new physics engine.

"Overachiever much?" I asked. "What made you decide to do both things at the same time? Just the physics engine is a huge advancement. I can't get my head around adding emergent gaming into that."

In emergent gaming, a character's decisions affected the outcome of the game. It was nothing new as a general concept, just cause and affect decision-making. Kick a puppy in the beginning, steal a weapon instead of buying it, and you'd find your character gradually becoming more evil as the game went on. But what Tate described had levels of subtlety, especially in the online portion of the game, that no one had achieved so far. *Syndrome* 2 could be the most realistic game ever created, both in terms of gameplay and the visual experience. It was incomprehensible that WGC had created both developments at the same time in the same game. Tate laughed self-consciously and shrugged.

"Holden had been messing around with ideas for the physics engine, and I'd been thinking about ways to make character decisions influence gameplay in a less linear way. We were doing this stuff on our own, and when we sat down to talk about what should be next, we couldn't decide, so we did both."

"You guys are nuts," I said, laughing.

"Yeah, we had a staff revolt when we made the announcement. But we hired some new engineers, and our people are amazing. *Syndrome 2* is going to be late, but when we finish it—"

"It's going to be the top-selling game of all time," I declared. Based on the short section I'd played, I knew that for a fact.

"That's the plan," Tate said.

"So, how did you guys end up running Mana? That seems completely random."

"Probably because it was," Tate said, and he went on to explain the series of events that had led to him and his cousin buying the nightclub. I never would've guessed it would be so easy to talk to him. Normally, being around a guy I found attractive left me tongue-tied, my heart pounding so hard I could barely breathe. I had a reaction to Tate, but even though he made my heart beat faster and my head spin, I didn't seem to have any trouble talking to him. After some of the dorky things I'd said, I wouldn't have minded being a little tongue-tied.

As Tate talked, I finished eating and ended up just staring at him, the way his dark hair fell in his eyes, the curve of his lower lip. His voice trailed off, and my eyes met his. The desire I saw there sent a jolt down my spine.

He'd caught me staring at his lips, and I was pretty sure I knew what he was thinking. My stomach fluttered, and I felt a prickle in my palms. I liked Tate. Like was such a tepid word. I didn't know how to describe the way I felt about Tate. Something in him drew me, pulled me out of myself, made me feel safe and thrilled all at the same time. I wanted more, even if I had only the vaguest idea what more would be. What would he expect? Dumb question. I had a pretty good idea what he'd expect.

At that thought, my stomach clenched and the prickle in my hands spread. My heart pounded in my chest so hard, I imagined I could hear it banging against my rib cage. I turned in the chair to face him, wanting to be closer to Tate, needing to ignore the panic rising inside me. I hadn't had an attack in a long time, and I was not going to have one with Tate. This isn't a panic attack, I told myself. It's just sensory overload. The best thing to do about that is to shut my brain off.

It felt like the craziest risk I'd ever taken, but I knew if I didn't do something, I was going to freak out, and I didn't want Tate to see me like that. Ignoring the thump of my heartbeat and the prickle in my palms, I leaned forward and pressed my lips to Tate's.

The second my mouth touched his, Tate took control. Kissing me, his lips coaxing mine open, he pulled me to my feet, backing me slowly away from the desk toward the couch on the far side of the room. I let him lead me, not caring where we were going as long as he kept kissing me. He fell backward onto the black leather couch, pulling me on top of him. The other times we'd kissed, Tate hadn't really used his hands. This time, he made up for it.

With my knees on either side of Tate's hips, my stretchy skirt rode up. Tate's hands closed over my thighs, pulling me down against him. I was mostly lost in the feeling of his mouth taking mine, but not enough to miss the length of his cock pressing against his jeans, nestled between my legs and right on my clit. If we hadn't been wearing so many clothes, he probably would've been inside me.

The thought made me shiver. I couldn't get my head around what was happening. Tate was kissing me, harder, deeper and far more thoroughly than he had before. I was on top, but I had no illusions as to who was in charge. His tongue stroked into my mouth, tasting me, and I couldn't help but answer the rhythm of our lips stroking and feeding on each other. It drove my already aroused body higher and hotter.

I ground down on his cock, through my underwear and his jeans. My breasts pressed into his chest, the padded push-up bra suddenly feeling too tight. I wanted it off. I wanted to be naked, my skin against Tate's. It wasn't enough just to feel his hands on my legs, first stroking my skin, then rising to grip my ass, rocking me against him.

Every time we came together, a wash of pleasure scattered my brain cells and made me gasp. It was too much, and I wanted more. When his fingers slid beneath my panties and grazed my clit, I tore my mouth from his and gasped, "Tate."

I was shaking. Jagged streaks of a pleasure so sharp it hurt raked through my body. I was wet where he touched me, slippery and hot. If I'd been more in control, I probably would've been embarrassed. Instead, my mouth dropped to Tate's neck, and I bit down, my fingers digging into his shoulders. A scream caught in my throat as he pressed one long finger inside my pussy.

I've never felt anything like this. With one hand on my ass, he urged me to rock against the hard length of his cock, rubbing against my clit. With the other, he fucked me with his finger. I was so tight, he only needed one. It didn't take long before I was coming, sobbing out his name against his skin.

The orgasm pulsed through me, my whole body squeezed tight, riding the wave of pleasure before it let go and I collapsed, breathing hard. A tear trickled from the corner of my eye, hot and wet on my cheek before it fell to Tate's neck.

I should have been relaxed. I'd never come before like that. Ever. I should've been a boneless mass of satisfaction. For a second or two, I was. Then I realized what had happened, what I'd done. Tate was still hard between my legs, and every conscious thought in my brain fizzed out, replaced by panic.

What was I supposed to do now? Stupid question. I could think of any number of things I should do, but my muscles wouldn't work. Paralyzed with indecision, I couldn't look at him. This had gone way too far, too fast, and I was lost.

Tate started to sit up, and the change in position got me moving. I eased off his lap, scrambling to my feet, frantically tugging my underwear back into place, and straightening my skirt, unable to meet Tate's eyes. Heat bloomed in my cheeks, and I knew I was blushing a bright red. Letting my hair fall over my face, I turned around, looking for my shoes. I had to go. I knew it was lame and stupid, and I was proving that I wasn't enough for him by running away, but I just couldn't do this. It was too much. Too much sensation. Too much that was new.

I could feel my thoughts getting away from me,

tumbling over themselves, screaming at me to run, to go, to get somewhere safe. I knew in my head that everything was okay. I was just freaking out. But an iron band of panic closed around my lungs until I couldn't breathe. My heart thundered in my ears. Tate was talking to me, and I could barely make out the words.

I grabbed my purse and keys from his desk and fled, tears streaming down my cheeks, the echo of his voice chasing me to the elevator, the sinking feeling of failure heavy in my heart.

CHAPTER EIGHT
EMILY

I don't remember getting home. Tate's office wasn't that far from my apartment, and I was practically running, so it couldn't have taken too long. When I got there, I locked the door behind me, dropped my purse and keys in the kitchen, and headed straight for my bed, curling up under the covers. I held my pillow tight to my chest, trying to stifle my sobs.

I *hated* this. I wanted to be anyone else. No, not anyone, just someone normal. Someone who could make out with a guy she liked and not completely freak out. Someone who could have a hook up and not make a total idiot of herself the way I had. I knew what had happened. While it hadn't been a full-blown panic attack, it was close enough, and I'd been there too many times not to understand how they worked. I'd been too wound up, already anxious, though a lot of that had been excitement and not fear. Still, I'd been on edge, and the sudden vulnerability of Tate's hands on me, of him making me come, was too much.

I understood how it had happened, but I shouldn't have run away. At that thought, I sobbed harder. I was a grown woman, not a teenager. I couldn't believe I'd run like a coward. There was no way Tate would want anything to do with me now, not when I'd proven how out of my league he really was. My phone beeped with a text, and I realized I still clutched it in my fingers.

You okay?

Tate. I was surprised he wanted anything to do with me. Shame and regret pulled me down, drowning the remains of my panic attack in a heavy blanket of sadness. I couldn't hide from him anymore. I'd run away after he'd taken the time to give me the most romantic date I'd ever imagined, and now he was checking on me to make sure I was all right. I owed him an explanation. At the thought of telling him why I'd run away, fresh tears streamed down my cheeks. It was enough knowing how badly equipped I was to handle normal life, but explaining my past, the anxiety attacks and agoraphobia to someone as successful and accomplished as Tate Winters was horrifying and depressing. I couldn't explain, but I had to apologize. Fumbling with my phone, I wrote,

I'm sorry.

I didn't know what else to say. 'Thank you for a nice dinner' didn't come close.

Tate texted back, *Are you at home? Are you okay?*

At home. Not really okay, I answered.

What happened?

And there it was. I wanted to blow him off so I wouldn't have to tell the truth. A lie would be so much easier. I couldn't bring myself to do it. I wasn't a good liar at the best of times, and Tate deserved better than that from me. He hadn't done anything wrong. I was the one who was fucked up. It wasn't fair to let him think this was his fault. Forcing my fingers to move, I wrote,

Sorry. It wasn't you.

I hit send and stared at what I'd written, knowing it wasn't enough. Sucking in a deep breath, I forced myself to keep going.

I have panic attacks.

I hit *Send* again, feeling as if I'd thrown myself off the side of a cliff, my stomach tight and nauseated, my ears ringing.

Was that a panic attack? In my office?

It was close, I admitted. *I'm sorry,* I typed again.

Don't be sorry, he answered almost immediately. *Can I call you? I want to talk to you.*

My first instinct was to say no, but that was always my first instinct when I felt this way. The panic made me want to pull the covers over my head and hide for the rest of my life. It was wrong. I knew that. Sometimes, saying *no* was the smart answer. This was not one of those times.

K.

A second later, my phone rang in my hand, sending a shock of sheer, icy panic through me. I squeezed my eyes shut for a second before I accepted Tate's call.

"Emily," he said, his voice unbearably gentle. "I'm sorry."

My breath hitched as I said, "No, I'm sorry. I'm sorry, Tate. It was a really nice date. The best date. I'm just fucked up. I'm not normal. I don't do normal things. I shouldn't have gone out with you. I should've known that would happen."

"Emily, no," he protested. "You're not fucked up. It's okay. We can try again."

I didn't know how to explain it to him. How to make him understand. "Tate, it's just too much. I don't know what we're doing. I don't know how to date someone. I just can't."

There was a long silence, so long that I wondered if he'd

hung up. I checked the screen of my phone and saw the timer on the call ticking upward. He was still there, just not talking. Finally, he said, "Don't give up on us. We'll figure it out. I think there's something good between us, and I don't want to walk away. We can take it slow. Slower. Whatever you need. Just don't give up."

I didn't want to give up. I wanted to try again. How long would it take before Tate got sick of dealing with me? Did it matter? If I walked away now, I wouldn't have him, anyway. I knew from experience that the only way to deal with my anxiety was to face it head on, no matter how awful it would feel.

I hadn't freaked out from spending time with Tate. I'd actually been surprisingly relaxed and at ease with him. It was the sex that had freaked me out. It had been too much, and I was too inexperienced. Tate was offering to go slow, but maybe slow was the opposite of what I needed. Maybe I needed to just suck it up and get it over with so the whole sex thing wasn't such a big, scary unknown. The thought grew in my mind. As crazy as it was, it felt right. I trusted Tate. He hadn't pushed me, and he'd said he was willing to be patient.

"Emily?" he asked, and I realized I'd been sitting there thinking for too long.

"We should have sex," I said in a rush.

"That's not taking it slow," Tate said, sounding confused. That made two of us.

"It's not sex itself that freaks me out," I tried to explain. "It's just that I haven't done it before."

"You haven't done it before?" Tate asked.

"No," I admitted. "I've been doing really well with the whole anxiety thing, but new things are always a problem. I don't know what I'm doing, and I think that's why I panicked."

"So you want to have sex as therapy?" His voice sounded funny, not like he was laughing, but tight and weird.

"Not just as therapy," I said. He probably though I was crazy.

"It's not that I don't want to sleep with you," Tate said, "because I really, really do. But I don't want to push you, or rush you, and jumping right into sex when it scares you seems like a very bad idea."

"I don't think it is, though," I said. "It's hard to explain."

"Try. I can't believe I'm saying this, but if you want us to have sex, you're going to have to give me a good reason we shouldn't wait."

"The short version is that the best way to deal with my panic attacks is to do the thing that scares me in a safe and controlled environment."

"We were in a safe and controlled environment tonight, weren't we?" he asked.

Any normal person would have thought so. "Not really, because I didn't know what was going to happen, and that was part of what set me off. If I know that we're going to have sex, that takes the uncertainty away. Does that make sense?"

"Kind of."

"So you'll do it?" I asked, half-hoping and half-terrified that he'd agree.

"When? Where?"

I thought about that. Soon, because I didn't want to give myself time to worry about it. Not at my apartment. There was a comfort level in being at home, but if I decided I wanted to leave and we were at Tate's, I could just go. I had a feeling it might be harder to get him out of my place if he wasn't inclined to leave.

"Tomorrow night," I said. "Your place."

"What time?"

"Eight." I said. I didn't want to make it like a date, so after dinner. But not too late.

"I'll see you at eight, then," Tate said.

"Okay. See you tomorrow," I said lamely. I hung up the phone, concluding what had to be the weirdest conversation of my entire life. Then I forced myself to get out of bed, wash my face, and put on my nightshirt. I was suddenly exhausted. I'd just propositioned Tate Winters, and in fewer than twenty-four hours, I was going to lose my virginity to him. It was crazy, but I knew without a doubt I wouldn't regret it. And maybe, if I didn't freak out and ruin it, we could try for something more.

CHAPTER NINE
TATE

The knock sounded on my door at 7:58. I'd worried that she might change her mind and bail on me. I'd been shocked as hell when she'd run out the night before. After our conversation, it made a bit more sense, but I was still out of my depth with Emily. I didn't know that much about anxiety or panic attacks, but if she was half as nervous as I was, we might be in trouble.

Crazy to say, with my history, but I'd never slept with a virgin before. I still couldn't get my brain around the idea that smart, beautiful Emily Winslow was untouched. Unfucked. How could a girl with a body like that—all soft curves, with that round ass and those full tits—hit her early twenties a virgin? Had no one bothered to break through her shyness? It seemed they hadn't.

I had the fleeting thought that I should bow out and leave her to a nicer guy, one who hadn't slept with so many faceless, nameless women. One who was as shy and sweet as Emily. That thought hadn't lasted long. She didn't need some mild-mannered guy to take her to bed. She needed me. I knew how to handle a body like hers. I'd make her come all night and fuck her until she couldn't walk. I'd make her mine.

Was that what I wanted? For her to be mine? To belong to me? I couldn't swear it, not yet, but I was pretty sure it was exactly what I wanted. It had taken all my willpower not to chase after her the night before when she'd run off. All my instincts had screamed that she was prey—all I had to do was catch her. I hadn't known about her panic attacks. I was thanking God that my gut—and Jo—had warned me to give Emily space. Chasing her down the street would have pushed her over the edge.

Jo said she was shy, but shy and having an anxiety disorder were not the same thing. If I'd known about the panic attacks, I might have done things differently. I'd followed her home at a distance, far enough that she couldn't spot me but close enough to see that she got back to her building safely.

Maybe I should've left her alone for the night, but I couldn't do it. I'd settled for texting her once I knew she was home, hoping at the very least to reestablish communication and keep her from shutting me out. I had not expected her proposition that we have sex. Don't get me wrong. I wanted sex with Emily. I could barely think about her without getting hard. But just going at it didn't feel right, not when our hooking up was the very thing that had almost sent her into a panic attack.

I could see her point, that taking it slow would just give her time to get nervous, and once she got it over with, it wouldn't be so intimidating. The way I saw it, my job was to show Emily how good she could feel when she was with me. I was starting to understand that her shyness and the panic attacks meant I'd have to handle her with care, but they had an unexpected upside. Once I'd had Emily in my bed, once

I'd shown her how much she wanted to be there, it was unlikely she'd look elsewhere. I'd gotten used to women who fucked anyone who caught their interest. I'm not judging. I did the same thing. Until now.

Emily had me thinking about more than just a random hookup. When I thought about Emily, I thought about time. Not just time in bed, though that mental image was becoming an obsession, but time with her. Emily was the first girl who caught my attention on every level. I wanted her body, and I loved to look at her. But she was more than that, more than her body, her face, her hair, and those crystal-clear gray eyes. She was smart, and a gamer. She was perfect for me. I just had to convince her that I was perfect for her.

I swung the door open at her hesitant knock, and my breath caught in my throat. Unlike the night before when she'd clearly dressed for a date, Emily wore faded jeans and a zip-front sweater that was attractive and well-cut but not the least bit seductive. Her gray eyes met mine, wary and skittish before landing on my shoulder. I thought I should let her take the lead, though it occurred to me that this might work better if I tossed her over my shoulder and carried her to my bedroom.

"Hey," she said.

"Come in." I stepped back from the open door to let her enter, closing and locking it behind her. She stood before me, her arms wrapped around her middle, each hand clutching the opposite elbow. Not the picture of a woman ready to be seduced.

I'd planned to let her take the lead, concerned about pushing her too far. I considered going the traditional route —a glass of wine, the right music—but we were beyond that. I'd tried that approach on our date, and it hadn't ended well.

I decided to step outside the box and take the direct approach.

"Which part makes you nervous?" I asked gently. "Is it having sex itself? Foreplay? I want to understand so I can make this good for you."

Emily visibly relaxed, her arms falling to her sides. She met my eyes, a sheepish expression on her face.

"This is embarrassing," she admitted. Trying to ease her mind and take the pressure off, I walked into my kitchen and grabbed a beer from the fridge, getting an extra for Emily. I popped them open, handed her the bottle, and leaned back against my counter, pretending I was completely chilled out about the conversation we were having. She was nervous enough on her own. She didn't need to know I was just as tense, afraid one wrong word would send her running again. I wasn't going to give up on Emily, but I knew we'd both be much happier if we could get past this now.

"Don't be embarrassed," I said. "We're going to figure this out together. I just need to know what it was last night that set off the panic. The way I touched you? How hard you came?"

I shifted against the counter, glad my jeans were loose enough to hide my hard cock. Just the memory of her coming, her tight pussy squeezing my fingers and her moans, had me on the edge. In response to my graphic questions, Emily's cheeks flushed a gorgeous deep pink. The color spread down her neck and over her collarbone. Were her tits that same shade of pink? I'd find out soon enough.

"It wasn't that," she said, her voice low and husky. She took a quick sip of her beer. "It was after. I didn't know what to do, and I started to worry that I was going to do something wrong, and then everything got tangled up in my head, and it was too much, and I started to panic."

I had to change the subject fast. I'd needed to know what set her off, but we weren't going to talk about it since that was clearly cranking her anxiety right back up to danger levels.

"So everything that came before was good?" I asked, loving how the flush in her cheeks deepened. Yeah, it had been good. Better than good. If I were being honest, feeling Emily Winslow coming on my fingers was better than the best sex I'd ever had. Knowing I was the first man to take her there, that mine were the first fingers inside that sweet pussy . . . there weren't words for how good that was.

Emily swallowed and nodded her head.

"Then I know what we're going to do," I said. "This first time, you don't have to do anything. If I need you to do something, I'll tell you. Or show you. You don't have to make any decisions, and nothing you do will be wrong."

"How do you know I won't do anything wrong?" She asked, her eyebrows knitted together in a frown.

"Because you couldn't possibly do anything wrong. It doesn't work like that. And I already know you're going to be a natural at this. You just need a little practice."

I set my beer on the counter and crossed the kitchen to Emily. I was giving her too much time to think. She didn't need her brain right now. She just needed to feel. I stopped in front of her and took the beer from her hands, setting it carefully on the counter behind her. She looked up at me those beautiful gray eyes clouded with worry and said, "How do you know I'll be good at it?"

"No one who kisses like you do could be anything but good in bed."

Her eyes brightened, and a small smile curved her lips

as she looked up at me. The contrasts in this woman were killing me. She was beautiful and brilliant, fun to be with, and filled with passion she hadn't yet tapped. She should have had all the confidence in the world, and when it came to her work, she did. But there was no reason a woman like Emily should be so uncertain when it came to her appeal. I'd never wanted anyone like this. There was no way I was just going to fuck her once and leave her. My normal MO was out the window. I didn't know where things were going with Emily and me, but getting her in my bed was going to be more than a one-time thing. If I could do this right, I could keep her there as long as I wanted.

I took her hands in mine and led her out of the kitchen, down the hall to my bedroom. I couldn't let myself touch her until we were near the bed. *Slow*, I reminded myself. *You have to take this slow.* I wasn't just worried about scaring her. I was terrified I was going to hurt her. I'd felt how tight she was the night before, and at the time, it had turned me on. It still turned me on, but my cock wasn't exactly small, or even average. I dreaded the idea of hurting her almost as much as I was desperate to get inside her.

My plan was simple. Get her so turned on, she couldn't think. We hadn't had any trouble with that part the night before. It was afterward when everything went to hell. This time, I knew what to look for. I looked down into Emily's face, meeting her eyes, falling into the clear gray, entranced at the way arousal and anticipation were chasing off her fears.

My fingertips light on her smooth skin, I brushed her hair back and tilted her face up to mine, touching my lips to hers in a light kiss. She let out the breath she was holding, scented with beer and mint. I ran my thumb over her full lower lip. She obediently opened for me. The mental image of her following other, kinkier orders flashed through my brain. *Slow*.

I kissed her again, tasting her with my lips and my tongue, wrapping my arms around her until her body was pressed to mine. Triumph surged through me when her hands wrapped around my back, her fists clenching in my shirt. She let out a little moan as I kissed her harder, losing myself in her mouth and the way she fit her body to mine.

Whatever went through her head when she got anxious, it wasn't a problem when I was touching her. I broke the kiss and our embrace just long enough to pull her shirt over her head. She acquiesced immediately, raising her arms and pulling them through the sleeves.

"I want to see you naked," I said. "Help me take your clothes off."

My hands went to the clasp of her bra. Hers dropped to the button of her jeans. With a rustle of fabric, her clothes hit the floor a second later, leaving her in nothing more than a pair of black lace panties. My mouth watered. Despite being black lace, they weren't overtly sexy panties—not a thong, and they didn't ride low on her hips. But on Emily, they were more than enough. Reminding myself for the millionth time to slow down, I scooped her up and carried her the few feet to my bed. Her eyelids were heavy as she stared up at me, her breath shallow as she let me lay her down on the dark comforter. I stripped off her black panties as I moved away, leaving her completely naked in my bed.

I stepped back to get rid of my own clothes, my mouth dry at the sight of Emily in my bed. Her long, dark hair gleamed in the dim light, and her creamy skin seemed to glow. Her body was almost too much. I wasn't used to women who looked like Emily, though I'd always been attracted to them. The women in my circles were groomed to within an inch of their lives, with perfect hair, perfect makeup and bodies surgically enhanced and incessantly exercised to drive off any hint of excess weight.

What they didn't get was that all that work would never outshine a woman as natural as Emily. Her legs were toned from walking, but her thighs and hips were full below the gentle rise of her belly, tapering to a waist that narrowed just below her un-fucking-believable breasts. No question— those were real. More than a handful, their weight pulling them to the sides, topped by small pink nipples drawn by arousal into tight little points. Except for her temptingly hard nipples, everything about Emily was rounded and soft and begged me to touch, invited my fingers to sink into her ass, her hips, and the back of her thighs as she straddled me and I fucked up into her tight, wet pussy.

Before she could start to think and get nervous, I joined her on the bed. Stretching out beside her, I took her mouth with mine, waiting until she relaxed into my kiss before touching her anywhere else. Patience had never been so hard before, but I'd never wanted to touch a woman as much as I wanted to touch Emily. When she moaned and rolled into me, I slid one hand down her back, around the curve of her ass to the back of her knee, and pulled her leg up over mine, opening her just a little. When my fingertips grazed the slick flesh between her legs, her breath caught and she let out a whimper. I hiked her leg higher and teased her with one finger, sliding it up and down, avoiding her clit, until her hips moved against me. I pushed my finger inside her, my balls drawing tight at the sucking clasp of her pussy. That was just one finger. I was going to have to stretch her out before I fucked her if I didn't want to hurt her. But first, I was going to make her come.

CHAPTER TEN
EMILY

I couldn't believe I was naked in bed with Tate Winters. When I'd freaked out the night before, I thought it was over. I'd been terrified I was going to mess things up again, right up until he kissed me. He'd known what he was talking about. Once he was touching me, I wasn't scared. I wasn't anxious. All I could do was feel, and I wanted more.

He pressed his finger inside me, and I squeezed my eyes shut, seeing sparks behind my closed lids, my head spinning at how good it felt. His finger was nothing like mine. It was thick and long, and I had the hazy thought that if one finger filled me up this much, I had no idea how his cock would fit. I trembled at the thought and let out a moan, sinking one hand into his thick, silky hair and kissing him harder. His thumb slid against my clit, and I ground my pussy against him, my body out of my control.

A second finger joined the first, the stretch just on the edge of pain. I leaned into him, raising my knee, opening myself further, as if that would make it easier to take his fingers. I thrust harder against him, my body finding its own

73

rhythm, chasing the pleasure of being so full. My head fell back, breaking our kiss, and I heard myself cry out as my orgasm hit. His fingers worked me through the waves of sensation, drawing out my release.

I wanted to give Tate the same pleasure he'd given me, and I reached down to close my fingers around his cock. I had the brief impression of length and impossible girth before he moved his hips back and said, "Not yet, baby."

Before I could worry that I'd done something wrong, he leaned in and kissed me, then said, "I want nothing more than your hand on my cock, but I'm way too close to the edge, and I want to fuck you, not come on your leg."

At his graphic language, I felt my cheeks heat. I used those words in my mind when I thought about sex, but somehow, that was nothing like hearing Tate say the word *cock* in his husky, aroused voice.

"I love the way you blush," he said, making my cheeks flame even hotter. "I was wondering how far down it would go."

He leaned back and stared at me, a satisfied smile on his face. His fingers were still inside me, and slowly, they started to move again. I squirmed against him. Abruptly, he slid his fingers from my body and sat up, stacking pillows against the headboard of his bed. He leaned back into them and tugged on my arm. Following his lead, I rose to my knees. I watched with wide eyes as he rolled on a condom. I really wasn't sure he was going to fit. Biologically, I knew it was possible, but still.

With his hands on my hips, he guided me to straddle him, positioning me so that the head of his cock was right against the gate of my pussy. He looked up at me and said, "I don't want to hurt you. This way, you can take your time with me while I distract myself with these perfect breasts."

Keeping his hands on my hips, he urged me down an inch, just enough so he was barely inside me, the stretch not too much more than his fingers but already giving me a taste of how big he was.

"Take your time, love." His hands left my hips and rose to my breasts, cupping their full weight, squeezing and lifting them. The look in his eyes, hot and absorbed, made me want to laugh even as it sent a bolt of heat between my legs. His fingers found my nipples, squeezing and pinching just hard enough, sending bolts of tingling bliss through my body. I wanted to move. I needed to move. And I realized *where* I wanted to move.

Down.

I wanted to take that thick, long cock inside my pussy and ride it. I wanted to make him come. And I wanted to come again, this time with more than his fingers inside me. I spread my knees a fraction and sank down, just a little, biting my lip at the pinch of pain as his cock pushed into my untried pussy.

Logically, I knew it was going to hurt the first time. Maybe if he'd been smaller . . . but I didn't want smaller. I wanted Tate. I could do this. I wiggled my hips from side to side, working my way down another inch, distracted by his hands kneading my breasts. When his mouth closed over one hard nipple, I let out a squeal that might have been embarrassing if I'd had enough operable brain cells to think about it. Instead of worrying about the sounds I was making, I arched my back, offering my breasts into his hands and sinking down another inch.

Lost to instinct, I dropped a hand between my legs and stroked my fingers over my clit, shocked at the intensity of the pleasure and thrilled at the feel of his cock partially buried inside me. I slid my fingers down his length and then back up, skating again over my clit and sinking a little farther down.

Tate groaned and said, "Jesus, fuck, but you're hot. Keep fucking doing that."

I did it again, my fingertips wet from my pussy, easily sliding over Tate's cock and up again to circle my clit. I did it over and over, each time taking more of him inside me until I had him to the root. I was stretched full, and it hurt, but I didn't fucking care, because it felt better than anything had ever felt in my entire life.

Tate raised his hips, thrusting up into me, and I fell forward, bracing myself on one hand. My nipple rested against his cheek, and Tate turned his head to take it, his hot mouth sucking hard. I rolled my hips into him, unable to stay still, rocking and grinding on him, hearing my own gasps and moans as if from a distance. It was too much, his mouth sucking my nipple, his cock so deep inside me, my hips moving, dragging my clit against him, everything swelling and rising until the pleasure crashed over me and I screamed out Tate's name.

The second my orgasm hit, Tate rolled me to my back, rising above me and fucking me hard, his hips pounding, his cock filling me to the hilt over and over. I held onto his arms and wrapped my legs around his hips, my eyes on his as the sharp, hot pleasure took me again, this time with Tate.

I don't know how long it was before I could catch my breath enough to say anything, and then when I could, I didn't know what to say. Everything that came to mind was inadequate. Amazing. Mind blowing. Stupendous. Best thing ever, and can we do it again? None of it was enough. I waited for the merry-go-round of thoughts that would lead me from concern to anxiety, but they didn't come. Every muscle in my body was relaxed. I was curled into Tate, my head on his shoulder, his arm tight around me and one leg thrown over my hip. Just as I was settling in, he kissed my forehead and said, "Be right back."

He returned a moment later, and I realized he'd been taking care of the condom. He slid into bed and pulled me back into his arms, tucking my head beneath his chin, his fingers stroking up and down my spine. "You okay?" he asked.

"Yeah, I'm good." I thought about it for a second. "I'm very good."

"Yes, you are," he said. I giggled, a lighthearted, silly sound. I couldn't remember the last time I'd giggled. I wasn't a giggler.

"So what do we do now?" I asked, feeling a little stupid but wanting to know. If Tate was waiting for me to leave, I didn't want to worry that I was missing his signals.

His arm tightened around me, and he said, "We stay right here until I get my breath back, and then we do it again."

"You want to cuddle and then do it again?" I asked, relieved that he wasn't trying to think of ways to get me to leave.

"Unless you want to go?" he said with a note of uncertainty in his voice that reassured me.

"No. I don't want to go, but you have to tell me . . . I don't—"

Tate gave me another squeeze and admitted, "I don't know what I'm doing here either. I don't usually cuddle women after sex."

"You don't?" I rose on one elbow to look down at him. His eyes were serious as they studied me.

"No. Normally, at this point, I'd be telling you about my early meeting or some other bullshit excuse to get you moving so you could go home. But I don't want you to leave. I want you to stay. This isn't just sex for me, Emily. I want more than that with you, and I can honestly tell you I've never said that to any woman before."

"Oh," I said, wonder spilling through my chest. I hadn't really thought Tate would want more with me. Part of me had assumed once we had sex, we'd be done. Tate brushed my hair off my face, his blue eyes searching mine.

"I want more too," I whispered.

Relief washed over his expression as he pulled me in for a kiss—a kiss that quickly got out of control. I was ready to have sex again, but Tate stopped me, saying, "You're too sore. You need a break. Let's try this instead."

He pulled me from the bed and led me into his bathroom, where he had an enormous soaking tub. I couldn't imagine Tate as the type who liked to take long baths, but the tub was more than big enough for the two of us. The short walk from the bedroom to the bathroom proved he was right. Despite the care he'd taken to get me ready and how much I'd enjoyed it, losing my virginity had left me raw and sore. Maybe I didn't want to have sex again just yet.

The tub filled quickly, and Tate settled me on top of him. We lay face-to-face, his already hard cock trapped between our bodies, pressing against my clit. He kissed me, and his mouth felt different, more possessive, as if it were claiming me. I liked it. I felt myself getting wet, my pussy softening, wanting his cock, leaking slick moisture. Instead of fucking me, he rocked against me, rubbing his hard cock against my clit, teasing both of us with the slippery pressure until the pleasure crested in a long, sweet orgasm. After, I collapsed against him, resting my head on his damp shoulder, knowing I never wanted to move.

"I haven't dry humped with a girl since I was a teenager," Tate said with a laugh after he kissed the top of my head.

"Is it still dry humping when we're in the tub?"

"Close enough."

We dried off and went back to bed, curling into each other as exhaustion finally hit and we fell asleep. The night was the best I'd ever had. I would have done it all over again, even knowing the nightmare we'd face when we woke up.

CHAPTER ELEVEN
EMILY

I woke up to late morning sunlight flooding Tate's bedroom, not as worried as I should have been that I was going to be late for class. I lay on my side, my head on Tate's chest and my arm wrapped around him. Slowly, I shifted to the side, not wanting to wake him, until I met his eyes and realized he was already awake.

"I probably should have gotten you up," he said, "but I was too comfortable to move."

On the bedside table, Tate's phone started to ring, a sugary pop song by a former child star turned singer. I raised an eyebrow at his ring tone choice, and he said, "Fucking Holden. He always does this."

"Are you going to answer?" I asked. Tate shook his head, levering his tall body out of the bed.

"No. He's probably just calling to tell me to get my ass into the office, which I will, as soon as I get you home. You have classes today?"

"All day, and game night tonight with my team," I said, pulling the sheet up to cover me, self-conscious in the bright light of day.

"Can I see you after?" He asked, his eyes level on my face. My answer mattered. He wasn't playing games with me, and I wouldn't play any with him.

"I can't skip game night. It's a thing—no one skips—but I can come over afterward."

"Works for me," Tate said. He disappeared into the bathroom, giving me a minute of privacy to find my clothes. I'd stashed extra underwear and a small toiletries bag in my purse. After our bath the night before, my hair was a mess, and I was grateful I at least had a comb and a hairband. I pulled on my clothes and bundled my hair into a messy pile on top of my head. It wasn't worth trying to take a shower at Tate's with my limited supplies. I'd wait until I got home. If we left in the next few minutes, I'd have just enough time to jump in the shower and change before I had to leave for class.

Fleetingly, I thought about staying in bed all day with Tate, but I dismissed it as impractical. It was clear from Holden's call that Tate had things to do, and I had too much scheduled on Wednesdays to bail with no notice.

Tate's phone rang again as we headed for the door, the same ring as before. I couldn't stop the laugh that bubbled out. The popular song was a favorite with the tween crowd. It was so not Tate.

"Are you sure you don't need to get that?" I asked.

"No, I'll see him as soon as I drop you off. Whatever he wants can wait."

Tate locked his door behind us and hit the button for the elevator. The doors slid open smoothly as if it had been waiting for us. Once inside, Tate took my hand in a firm grip and tugged me close, wrapping his arms around me, tucking my head beneath his chin. We stood there in silence as we descended to the garage level, not needing to speak.

My nerves from our first date were gone, washed away by Tate's easy acceptance of my fears and his honesty about his feelings for me. A relationship with him wasn't going to be easy—nothing new was ever easy for me—but after the night we'd shared, I was beginning to believe we could make it work.

The elevator arrived at the garage level with a gentle bump, the doors sliding open soundlessly. Tate took my hand again, leading me through the doors and into my worst nightmare.

Lights flashed in my eyes as voices shouted Tate's name, a mass of bodies pushing and shoving in their rush to get to us. Tate stepped in front of me, using one arm to hold me behind him as he tried to push us through the crowd.

"Tate, who are you with?"

"Tate, what do you think about Jacob being attacked? Is he involved with organized crime?"

"Tate, can you tell us what happened here earlier?"

A hand grabbed my arm and tried to pull me away from Tate. I yanked my arm back and came face to face with a woman in a red suit, shoving her camera in my face, the flash blinding me as she took picture after picture. Nausea swelled in my stomach. I was nine years old again, trying to go the school, my path blocked by a crowd of vultures shouting at me.

Emily, are you happy the gunman is dead?

Emily, how do you feel about watching your best friend die?

Emily, how does it feel to be the only one left alive?

Emily!

Emily!

The memories cascaded, tangling with the present, drowning me in the attack of lights and voices. The yelling blurred into one voice, shouting over and over. My heart pounded in my ears, racing, beating so fast I felt light-headed. My palms prickled with sweat, and it felt like an iron band was cinching closed around my chest. I couldn't breathe. My vision was going gray.

I felt Tate pulling me through the garage, moving me away from the crowd of reporters. As if far off in the distance, I heard other voices, saw figures in black blocking the crowd from us, ushering them back to wherever they'd come from.

It didn't matter. It was too late for me. It was already starting. A door opened, and then I was sitting. In a car. I was in a car. We were moving, and all I could think about was getting air into my frozen lungs. I leaned over, wrapping my arms around my knees, burying my face between them. I didn't want this to happen. I was not going to let this happen.

I hadn't had an anxiety attack in over a year. I'd told myself I was done with them. I might have been if I hadn't been confronted with the very thing that had started me down this path in the first place. No normal woman would be assaulted by reporters on a regular basis. This wasn't because of me. This was because of Tate. Nausea hit me in another surge, and I bit down on my lip, desperate not to throw up in Tate's car. We were safe. We were away from the flashing lights and screaming voices, but in the back of my mind, all I could hear was the warning that I was in danger.

I wasn't in danger. I knew that. I struggled to draw breath, to calm my racing heart. I could feel myself shaking, feel the sweat running down my back and gathering under my arms. My body was out of my control, taking me on a ride more terrifying than any roller coaster. I tried to remember everything I'd learned in therapy.

Deep breaths. I needed to breathe and stop the merry-go-round of panic in my mind. I told myself everything I knew I needed to hear.

I'm okay. The reporters can't hurt me. Everything is going to be okay.

It was dizzying, being tossed back into the nightmare that had haunted me since I was a child. I'd been dealing with the anxiety attacks. I'd gotten so much better. I should have known this could happen, being with Tate. But I hadn't been thinking. I liked him so much, and I'd wanted him. If I'd thought it through, really considered what I was doing, this wouldn't be happening. I should have known. I should have kept myself safe.

By the time the car slowed and pulled to a stop, I was mostly under control. My heart was still beating way too fast, and I was shaking, but at least I didn't think I was going to pass out or throw up. Tate reached down to help me out of the car, and I gripped his hand, desperate for an anchor. I let him wrap his arm around me and guide me into my building. At my door, he said, "Do you have your keys, baby?"

I fumbled in my purse until the cool metal scraped my fingers and dragged them out, shoving them at Tate. My hands were shaking too hard to get them in the lock myself. The door swung open, and I heard Jo say, "Emily! What happened? Tate, what's going on?"

I pulled away from Tate, trying to stand on my own. A sudden wave of dizziness hit me and my stomach pitched. I wasn't going to pass out, but I was going to throw up. Mouth watering, sweat pouring down my face, I tore my hand out of Tate's and lurched down the hallway, falling to my knees in front of the toilet just in time to empty my stomach. I was still heaving, the muscles in my abdomen clenching and twisting in painful cramps, when I felt him behind me. His warm hand landed on my clammy back, and I flinched.

A part of me wanted to crawl into Tate's lap and let him fix everything. But he couldn't fix this. I was broken, and no matter how good I got at handling my anxiety problems, the media circus was always going to be a part of Tate's life. A tiny sliver of me resented him for it. It wasn't fair to resent him for my problems. I knew that. But kneeling on the bathroom floor, puking up my guts after being ambushed by reporters and fighting back flashbacks from the worst part of my childhood, I didn't care about fair. I just wanted to go back to being okay.

"Go away," I rasped. "Go away, please, Tate."

After a minute, he did, leaving me alone.

I don't know how long it took me to get myself together, but eventually, I got up off the floor. I was still a sweaty, shaky mess, and I couldn't stand it a second longer. I turned on the shower almost hot enough to burn and stood under the steamy spray, letting my mind drift.

Tate was still there when I came out, my hair combed straight, bundled in a thick fuzzy robe. His eyes flashed to me, dark with worry. He started toward me, then stopped.

"Are you okay?" he asked, reaching out a hand, then dropping it to his side when I kept my distance. Jo looked between us, frowning, and said,

"I made you some tea." She set a mug on the kitchen table, and I lowered myself into a chair, feeling ancient. After an episode like that, every muscle in my body hurt. I was exhausted, and I wanted to be alone, but I had to do this first.

"Can you sit down?" I asked, looking up at him. The

expression on his face, worry mixed with frustration, made me want to cry. I fought it back. I needed to keep it together long enough to talk to Tate. Once that was done, I was going to crawl into bed and cry myself to sleep.

"Was that a panic attack?" he asked gently.

"Yeah," I said. "I haven't had one in over a year."

"Was it the reporters?" Tate asked, looking at Jo and then back at me. Then she hadn't told him. Jo was the best, and she knew how to keep a secret.

"When I was nine, I went on a play date with my best friend," I said. Tate looked confused. I didn't blame him, but I didn't know how else to do it. I had to tell the story, and then he would understand. "It was a day off school, a teacher workday or something, and Kelly's mom took us to one of those arcades for kids with the cartoon animals and the pizza. We were there about an hour when a man came in and started arguing with a woman who worked there. He was her ex-husband. They'd been fighting over custody, but I didn't know any of that. I just heard the yelling, and it scared me. I was in the ball pit with Kelly. She ran for her mom, but I hid in the balls. The woman was screaming back at him, and he hit her. When she got back up, he pulled out a gun. He started shooting. He didn't stop until everyone was dead. I was the only one who survived. I hid in the bottom of the ball pit, and I didn't come out until the police found me."

"Emily," Tate said, his voice heavy with pain and the horror of what he'd heard. His hands reached across the table for mine, but I sat back, gripping the warm mug of tea. I wanted his comfort. Half of me wanted to burrow into him and let him wrap his strong arms around me and keep me safe. The other half couldn't forget that he was the reason we'd been ambushed by the reporters in the first place.

They hadn't been shouting my name. They'd been shouting Tate's.

"They wouldn't leave me alone," I said, wanting to finish it. "They followed me everywhere, the reporters, taking my picture and yelling at me. They waited in the street outside my school." I shook my head as if trying to banish the memories.

"I didn't start having the panic attacks until later. I don't know, maybe it took time for everything to filter through. But it started then, at the shooting and right after."

I looked down at my cup of tea and took a long sip. When I thought I had enough courage, I looked back up at Tate and said, "I can't do this with you. I want to. I do. But I can't. I can't face that kind of attention. I won't be able to handle it."

"Emily, don't. That doesn't happen all the time. It doesn't even happen often. Something is going on with my cousin, Jacob—that's what it was about. It wasn't even me. We can handle this."

"No, we can't," I said, feeling sick and hopeless. "I can't. I worked so hard to get here, to have a life that was even close to normal. Now I feel it all sliding away. I've gone a year without having any panic attacks, and now I've had two in three days."

"You said the other day wasn't a panic attack," Tate argued.

"I have too much at stake, Tate," I said. "I don't want to go back to how I was before, living at home, scared to leave the house. I'm better off alone. I'm sorry."

"So that's it? Just *I'm sorry*, and it's over?" Tate shoved back out of his seat and stood, glaring down at me.

"You don't understand," I said. "You don't understand how bad I was and how hard it was to get better. I care about you. I care about you a lot. But I can't do this, Tate. I can't."

I was so tired. My head hurt, and I still felt queasy. I risked a look at Tate and immediately wished I hadn't. His deep blue eyes were dark with anger, his arms crossed over his chest. Maybe being mad at me would make this easier for him. I didn't want to hurt Tate. That was the last thing I wanted, but I'd been crazy to think I could make a relationship with him work. With another guy, maybe— someone low-profile who lived a quiet life. I couldn't handle Tate Winters. This morning had proved it without a doubt.

Suddenly desperate to end the whole thing, I got up from the table and said, "I'm sorry," before turning and fleeing down the hall to the safety of my bedroom.

Jo came in a few minutes later and sat on the edge of my bed.

"You need to get some rest," she said. "Sit up and let me braid your hair so it doesn't get all tangled."

I did, turning my back to her, and felt my tight muscles relax under the soothing strokes of the comb against my scalp, the tug of it pulling on my hair. She sat there and combed my hair, waiting for me to calm down. Finally, she gathered the wet strands and began to braid them.

"Are you sure about this, Em?" she asked quietly.

I sighed. I didn't want to be sure. I wanted Tate. But just the memory of the shouting reporters and the flashing lights was enough to remind me that it couldn't happen.

"No," I said honestly. "But I can feel myself falling apart, Jo. Everything has been so good, but since I met Tate, I feel like I'm sliding closer and closer to the edge. It scares me," I whispered.

"I know," Jo said. "But you need to think about this,

Emily. He really cares about you. He wasn't just mad when you made him leave. He was hurt."

A tear slid down my cheek. The idea of hurting Tate was a knife in my heart. I cared about him—more than I should, when we'd known each other for less than a week.

"I know you're scared," Jo went on. "And you need to do what's right for you. But Emily, don't think about what's right for you from a place of fear. How did your therapist help you get over your agoraphobia?"

It sounded like a random question, but I knew what Josephine was getting at. "I had to do the things that scared me," I said in a low voice. "But this is different."

"How is this different, Em?" She tied off the braid and urged me to lay down on the bed, pulling my quilt up around my shoulders and stroking my forehead. "Get some rest. I know that scene was a nightmare. The only person who feels worse about it than you is Tate."

She left quietly, and I pulled the quilt around me, clutching it with my fingers, tears rolling down my cheeks. Jo was right. I knew she was right. I was still in a cage, a bigger cage than I'd been in a few years ago, but I was still trapped by my own fears, and the only way to beat them was to face them. This time, the reward wasn't college or a career. If I could find the courage, the reward could be Tate. If he still wanted me.

CHAPTER TWELVE
TATE

I pounded on the door of Jacob's apartment, furious that he hadn't answered. I knew he was home. He wasn't in his office, my first stop, and Holden had told me he was no longer with the police. I wished, more than anything, that I'd answered Holden's calls that morning. He'd been trying to warn me about the reporters, and if I'd known, I could've told Emily, and I would have found out what a big fucking problem they would be.

Instead, I walked into that cluster fuck blind and ended up losing Emily. Maybe it was my fault. I hadn't tried hard enough to talk her around, or been patient enough, but at that moment, I was happier blaming Jacob.

I had a key to Jacob's door, though he'd probably rip my head off if I used it. I didn't care. Let him get pissed. I could use a fight.

I unlocked the door and swung it open, revealing the front hall of Jacob's plush penthouse. My cousin owned the top floor of Winters House, and it looked like a gilded age mansion with gleaming hardwoods, smooth, creamy plaster walls, and priceless oil paintings. To my surprise, a woman stood in front of me, her dark hair up in a twist, dressed in yoga pants and a matching tailored hoodie, holding Jacob's house phone up as if it were a weapon. Her eyes went wide at the sight of me, and she backed up a step. In a calm, cultured voice, she said, "Leave, or I'm calling security."

"Who the hell are you? And what are you doing in my cousin's penthouse?" I demanded.

She narrowed her eyes on my face, studying me for a moment before her shoulders relaxed and she dropped the hand holding the phone. "You're one of Jacob's cousins, I presume? Which one? You're too young to be Gage, or Vance, so you must be Tate."

She was clever, whoever she was. "Good call. When will Jacob be back?"

"You'd better come in," she said, turning and disappearing into the penthouse. I followed her, curiosity beginning to outweigh my frustration.

"Who are you?" I asked again as she came to a stop in Jacob's kitchen.

"I think it's better if Jacob answers that question. But I have his permission to be here, if that's what you're worried about. Would you like some coffee? Tea? It's a little early for lunch, but I can probably throw something together."

"Coffee, and something to eat, if you have it. It's been a long morning," I said, sitting down at the counter facing the rest of the kitchen. The woman moved as if she were very familiar with her surroundings, starting coffee and pulling things out of the fridge. This was beyond weird. If Holden was touchy about letting women in his apartment, Jacob was even worse. He was occasionally open to houseguests— a few months ago, he'd sheltered a friend of the family's girlfriend when she was having a hard time—maybe this was something similar. There was no way she was involved with

Jacob. He'd never let a woman he was fucking live in his house. Still, she was exactly his type, classically beautiful, polished and elegant despite her casual clothes. Her hands moved with grace as she assembled a sandwich. Something about her tugged at my memory, and I had the feeling I was missing something.

"Do I know you?" I asked.

"Wouldn't you know if you did?" she countered. "Cream? Sugar?" She held up a steaming mug of coffee.

"Black is fine." I took the coffee and sipped, grateful for the caffeine.

"Did the mess in the parking garage this morning have anything to do with you?" I asked, fishing for information. The woman flinched but recovered immediately, her face shifting back to the same calm, serene expression.

"You really need to ask Jacob. He called half an hour ago and said he was on his way home."

I drank my coffee, understanding that as polite as Jacob's guest was, she wasn't going to tell me anything. Holden hadn't known why there had been police and reporters in the parking garage either. He'd gotten a call from Cooper Sinclair, telling him to stay in the office and keep his head down—and to call me—but that was it.

The woman slid a turkey sandwich in front of me, and I ate it gratefully, noting as I did the thin layer of pesto and the fresh tomatoes. So Jacob didn't just have a woman living with him. He had one who could cook. Good to know. She'd excused herself while I was eating, leaving me alone in Jacob's kitchen. Annoyed at the wait, I wandered around when I was finished eating, ending up in Jacob's office. Like everything else, it was old school, elegant, and very neat. Jacob was wound way too tight to leave things lying around. I was curious to see a manila envelope left on his desk, the clasp open and papers pulled halfway out. I didn't think I'd ever seen anything on his desk aside from the blotter and pen.

Bored and feeling nosy, I picked it up and looked at the photograph on top only to freeze in shock. With a shaking hand, I withdrew the photograph. It showed a room I'd only seen in pictures and a woman I barely remembered sprawled on an oriental carpet, her hand flung above her head, a bullet wound in her chest. What the fuck? Grief, old and sour, weighed on my heart. I'd seen this picture once and had never wanted to see it again. I barely remembered my mother. I didn't want this ugly image of her dead body in my head, crowding out the few memories I had of her when she was still alive.

"Put that down," Jacob said from behind me, reaching around to yank the envelope and the photograph out of my hands.

"Why do you have that?" I asked, confused and a little sick. "Why do you have a crime scene picture of my parents' murder? What the fuck is going on? Does this have anything to do with what happened downstairs? And why do you have a woman living with you that none of us have ever seen?"

"Would you relax?" Jacob asked, his voice ice cold, his tone suggesting I do as he said or face the consequences.

"No, I will not relax. I want to know what's fucking going on. My girlfriend just broke up with me over that bullshit in the garage."

Jacob's eyes softened, but he raised a sardonic eyebrow and said, "Your girlfriend? Since when do you have a girlfriend?"

Feeling annoyingly put in my place, I shoved my hands

in my pockets and said, "Since this morning, but it didn't last very long, thanks to you."

Jacob went around to the other side of his desk and shoved the envelope and picture in a drawer, slamming it shut. "I'm not going to talk about the picture. Not yet. Come back in the kitchen," he said. "It's been a long fucking morning, and I'm starving."

"Fine." I followed him back to the kitchen, where the woman, now wearing a linen shift dress and sandals, was making Jacob a sandwich similar to the one she'd made for me. Looking between her and my cousin I said, "Are you going to introduce us?"

I wasn't expecting to see Jacob walk up behind her and slide his arm around her waist, dropping a gentle kiss on her neck just below her ear. She murmured something to him and he answered, but I couldn't hear what they said.

"Abigail, you've met my cousin, Tate. Tate, this is Abigail Jordan. She's my guest, and while she's here, security has been tightened."

"It's nice to meet you, Abigail," I said, smiling at her. To Jacob, without a smile, I said, "Where have you been all morning? What happened in the garage?"

Jacob took the coffee Abigail handed him and sipped before he said, "Abigail had an unfortunate situation that is none of your business. As part of that situation, someone tried to shoot me in the garage this morning. We're still not sure exactly how he got in, but he's in police custody and I'm fine. When she got here, I increased security, but I did it quietly because we didn't want to broadcast her location. After this morning, that's no longer a concern."

"The Sinclairs are on it?" I asked. Jacob nodded.

"You, Holden, and the other residents will get a brief this afternoon. Traffic in and out of the garage will be personally checked. It's going to be slow, but it should prevent the kind of scene you dealt with this morning."

"And you're not going to tell me why someone was shooting at you?" I asked.

Abigail started to speak, but Jacob flashed a glance in her direction and she stopped, biting her lip as if to prevent any sound from leaking out.

"It's not your business," Jacob repeated. "Despite what happened this morning, I don't want anyone to know Abigail is here, so don't tell Holden or your brothers."

Wanting to mess with him a little, I said, "What about your brothers?" I knew that if Abigail were a secret, he definitely wouldn't want Aidan to know. Aiden was the oldest of all of us, the patriarch of the family now that our parents were dead, and he was both nosy and bossy. If Abigail was a secret, Jacob definitely wouldn't want Aidan to know about her. Showing signs of temper for the first time, Jacob said, "Don't fucking tell Aidan anything."

Interrupting us, Abigail asked, "Your girlfriend broke up with you because of what happened in the garage?"

"Because of the reporters," I said. "They were like a pack of wolves, shouting and taking pictures. Emily has problems with anxiety and panic attacks, and it was too much. She freaked out, and then she broke up with me."

Jacob didn't say anything, just narrowed his eyes, but Abigail frowned and considered before she said, "Did she freak out, or did she have a panic attack?"

"She had a panic attack," I admitted. "It was pretty bad." So bad, I couldn't get it out of my head. Her face had been white, sweat pouring down her skin, her body shaking so hard she could barely stand up. Listening to her struggle to breathe on the short car ride to her apartment had been torture.

"I had a friend in college who had panic attacks," Abigail said quietly. "I always felt terrible for her when they happened."

Somehow, Abigail's quiet acceptance made me feel the need to explain. "Emily was a victim in a mass shooting when she was a kid, the only survivor, and the media was relentless. She said the panic attacks started because of that."

"We know what that's like," Jacob said, meeting my eyes. We did know. The attention had been brutal when Jacob's parents had died. I didn't remember the fallout from losing my own mother and father, but losing my aunt and uncle had been hellish—both the sudden loss and the unrelenting harassment by the media. At least we'd had each other to lean on, to buffer the intensity. Emily had been on her own, dealing with survivor's guilt on top of everything else.

"Walking into that garage this morning must have been horrible for her," Abigail said. "Is she all right?"

I shook my head. "I don't know. She told me she couldn't deal with me anymore and kicked me out."

"She kicked you out? And you just left?" Jacob demanded. I heard the censure in his voice, but he hadn't seen Emily. The last thing I'd wanted to do was push her when it was taking everything she had to hold herself together. She'd asked me to go, so I'd gone.

"You don't understand," I said, echoing Emily's comment to me.

"So what are you going to do?" Jacob asked. "Or is this going to be the shortest relationship in the history of relationships?"

"What am I supposed to do?" I asked, irritated. It wasn't like Jacob was a relationship expert. He rotated through the same group of socialites, but he never kept any of them around for long. I'd never seen him display the kind of easy affection he'd showed Abigail.

"I don't know," Jacob said, sarcasm dripping from his words. "Go apologize? Beg her forgiveness and tell her you can work things out? Or is her condition too much and you don't want to deal with it?"

"It's not too much," I protested. "But I can't force her to want to be with me. And she's right, we do have to deal with the media. I can try to keep her safe from that, but I can't make any promises. I won't lie to her."

"Do you love her? Or are you just having fun?"

"We haven't been together that long," I said, wishing I knew the answer to his question. "I've never been in love before. I know I don't want to lose her. I've never felt like this about any woman. I just don't know how to fix this."

"Tell her how you feel," Abigail said softly. "Be honest with her and tell her how you feel. She had a shock this morning, and she probably regrets breaking up with you. I'd give her a little space to get over the panic attack, but not too much, and then go talk to her."

I leaned against the counter and looked down at my feet, thinking. There had to be a way to work this out with Emily. I couldn't let her go. I wouldn't put her in a situation that was bad for her, wouldn't ask her to subject herself to the kind of thing that happened this morning. But we would find an answer. What we had was too good to throw away.

CHAPTER THIRTEEN
EMILY

I stopped at my front door, my hand on the knob, checking my back pocket for my keys as I balanced a wicker basket in the crook of my arm. The basket hadn't seemed that heavy when I was packing it, but now that I was carrying it, I realized I'd misjudged. Fortunately, I didn't have that far to go. It had been two days since I'd seen Tate. Two very long days. I missed him, missed him so much my heart hurt just thinking about it, but I'd had to do some thinking, then some talking, and after that, more thinking. Now it was time to act.

I left my apartment, locking the door behind me. It was time to talk to Tate. I wasn't sure he was home, but I'd try there first, even if it meant pushing my way through more reporters. Jo had told me that interest had calmed down, but there were still a few of them trolling the street in front of the building, looking for a story. She still didn't know what had happened. No one did, not really, but that wasn't stopping the papers from trying to tie Tate's cousin, Holden's brother, Jacob, to organized crime and gang violence. The whole thing was nuts. I was so absorbed in thinking about

Tate and the drama at Winters House, I almost walked into the door to the stairwell when it swung open.

Taking a quick step back, I looked up and met Tate's dark blue eyes. "I was coming to see you," I said nervously, shifting the basket from one arm to the other. He eyed it, then looked at me.

"You were?" He stepped into the hallway and let the door shut behind him. "Can we go to your apartment? I have some things to say."

I nodded and turned around, fumbling for my keys. It reminded me of the last time we'd been at my door together. I'd put a lot of the blame for my panic attack on Tate, but that hadn't been fair. The reporters may have been calling his name, but he hadn't been the reason they were there. And he'd gotten me away from them safely, had taken care of me when he didn't even know what was wrong.

I let us in, putting the basket on the kitchen table. "Do you want anything? Beer? Coffee?" I asked, feeling awkward. Tate shook his head.

"Can we sit down?" He went to the couch, and I followed, my carefully rehearsed speech falling apart in my head. I'd planned what to say, had a list of points I'd wanted to make, and now, I couldn't remember a single one. I joined Tate on the couch, my knees pressed together, trying to think of what to say.

At a loss, I finally blurted out, "I'm sorry."

"Why are you sorry?" Tate asked in surprise. "You didn't do anything wrong. I'm the one who needs to apologize. If I'd answered Holden's call, none of that would have happened."

I shook my head. "It's not your fault I have anxiety attacks, Tate. And it's not your fault I had that one. It's just something I have to deal with. Even before the shooting, I was shy. I've never liked attention. I've gotten much better, but I don't know that it's ever going to completely go away."

"What does that mean for us?" he asked, moving closer and taking my hand in his, lacing our fingers. I looked down and closed my fingers around his, gripping them tightly.

"I don't know," I answered as honestly as I could. "I care about you. A lot. More than I should, considering I don't really know you that well."

"I feel the same way." Tate reached out and tilted my face up to his. "I can't stand the idea of losing you, Emily. You fit with me. I don't care about the rest of the world. When I'm with you, everything feels right. Whatever we have to do to make this work, we can do it. If you don't want to come to my building, I'll move. There are family events I can't avoid, but you don't have to deal with anything you don't want to."

I let out a breath I hadn't realized I'd been holding. "I don't want you to move, Tate." A half-laugh escaped me, and I shook my head. "I saw my therapist yesterday—talked to her about how I was feeling. It helped me clarify some things."

"And?" Tate asked.

"She reminded me that getting better is about facing my fears, not running from them. I'm never going to be okay with the kind of thing that happened yesterday. And I don't think I'm going to love the idea of going to events where there are a lot of reporters. But if you're willing to be patient while I work on getting better, I want to try."

"It's not about patience, Emily," Tate said. "I want to be with you. I want you to be happy, and I'll do whatever I have to do to make that happen. You only have to tell me what you need."

"You," I said. "I just need you. If you can stand by me

while I keep trying to handle this, that's all I want. A chance to be with you."

In answer, Tate pulled me close, his lips taking mine with a desperation I hadn't felt before. I matched it with my own. Two days apart felt like a year. I'd been so scared I'd ruined everything by pushing him away. I fell back into the couch cushions, Tate on top of me, loving the weight and heat of his long body pinning me down. I ran my fingers through his hair, holding his hand, kissing him back with everything I had. When his hand slid under my shirt, I broke the kiss and said,

"I made you a picnic."

Tate sat up, pulling me with him. "You made me a picnic? You can cook?"

"I can cook," I affirmed. "I'm not going to get any Michelin stars, but I made lasagna, garlic bread, and a double chocolate cake."

He looked at the basket on my kitchen table. "You were bringing me a picnic?"

"I want to eat it at your apartment. Tonight."

Tate understood what I was saying. "You don't have to go back there, baby. We can wait."

"No," I said firmly. I loved that Tate wanted to protect me. I'd probably come to depend on it, to depend on the knowledge that I had someone who would try to keep me safe at all costs. But there were some things I had to do, especially *because* they were hard. "That's your home, Tate. Your family is there. I have to be able to go back."

"You were going to bring me the picnic? What if there had been reporters?" he asked.

"I would have dealt with it. I needed to see you."

He stood, his hand gripping mine. "I drove over here."

"It's okay." I said, then paused. "Are there still reporters in the garage?" I was going to push myself to face my fears, but I wasn't ready to dive back into my nightmare.

"No reporters," Tate promised. "Jacob has security all over the building, including the garage. No one gets in unless they've been personally vetted. I'll have you added to the system so you can drive in the garage and come straight to my place."

"Then let's go," I said. "The sooner we have dinner, the sooner we can get to desert."

I won't lie. My stomach flipped over when we drove into the garage. At the sight of the elevator and the spot where the reporters had ambushed us, my heart sped up. I took deep breaths and held Tate's hand, reminding myself that I was safe until the elevator doors slid shut and we were moving away from the garage.

"You okay?" Tate asked, kissing the top of my head. I smiled, resting my cheek against his chest.

"You don't have to keep asking," I said carefully. "I don't want you to be worried about me all the time. I don't want to be a burden."

"Humor me. And you're never going to be a burden. Don't talk about yourself that way."

"You say that now—" I started. Tate cut in.

"We both have things in our lives that aren't easy. It makes me a little crazy that I can't protect you from the media," Tate confessed. "I want to promise you that they'll never bother you again, but I can't. I can arrange security, protect you with all my resources, but that's no guarantee."

"I know that, Tate. I do." I unpacked the picnic basket, putting the lasagna in the oven on warm. I had other things on my mind than food. First, I had to make things right with Tate. "I overreacted the other day. I'm sorry."

"You didn't overreact. You had a panic attack." He leapt to my defense so quickly, it brought tears to my eyes.

"I didn't mean the panic attack. I meant blaming you. Asking you to leave." He looked away, and I realized all over again how much I'd hurt him. Crossing the kitchen, I got in his space, demanding his attention. "I was wrong," I said firmly. "That wasn't your fault. You can't promise that mess won't happen again. And I can't promise I'll be able to handle it when it does. But I can promise I won't bail on you. I won't blame you. The next time we have a disaster, we'll stick together."

"Damn straight," he said. The raw emotion in his deep blue eyes stole my breath. He stared down at me, his eyes locked on mine as if he were unable to break our connection. I could have stayed there forever, face to face, wrapped in Tate's embrace, falling into his eyes. It was too soon to call this love. Wasn't it? I didn't know. With Tate, I was on completely new ground. I had no idea what we were doing, what labels to put on it. I only knew that all I wanted was Tate.

I rose on my tiptoes and tilted my head back, sliding my lips over his in a soft kiss. "I'm not sore anymore," I murmured, my lips rubbing his with each word. "And I bought new underwear."

I shrieked in surprise as Tate's hands closed over my waist and he lifted me, tossing me over his shoulder in a fireman's carry. Before I could get my breath, the world turned upside down and I was bouncing on his mattress, looking up into blue eyes heavy with desire.

"Let me see," he demanded. Always happy to follow Tate's orders, I stripped off my shirt to reveal an almost sheer black lace bra. "Now the rest."

I peeled down my jeans, leaving me in nothing but the

bra and its matching thong. Tate's eyes flared wide. "This too?" I asked, hooking my thumb under the strap of the bra.

"I'll get that." He flicked the clasp of the bra, leaning back to watch it slide down, the straps catching on my elbows. I thought he was going to take it off, but he twisted the fabric around my arms, trapping them as he pulled my wrists over my head and lowered me to the mattress. "Stay there," he ordered.

"Yes, sir," I whispered. I meant for the words to sound ironic, but they came out breathy. I couldn't help it. Tate ordering me around when I was mostly naked was hot. Beyond hot. It was nuclear.

He arranged my legs on the bed, spreading them wide. My skin was flushed, my back arching, instinctively trying to draw his attention to my breasts. The room was warm, but my nipples jutted, diamond hard and a dark pink. My body wanted Tate. Every part of me wanted him. I wanted him to fuck me. I wanted to lay with him in the tangled sheets afterward. I wanted to watch him eat the dinner I'd cooked. I wanted everything.

He stripped off his clothes in quick, efficient move-ments, displaying his athletic body to my hungry eyes. A pulse of heat between my legs made me squirm. I was already wet, and we hadn't done anything yet. At the sight of his hard cock, thick and long, I drew in a breath. I still couldn't believe it had been inside me.

A second later, he was kneeling between my legs, a condom in hand, looking down at me, his gaze traveling over my mostly naked body, taking in every detail. He reached out a hand and touched my shoulder, his fingertips a brand on my skin, burning. Claiming. They traveled over my body, stroking my collarbone, circling one breast, then the other, rounding my ribcage to dip in my belly button, leaving a trail of fire in their wake. It took everything I had not to move, but I sensed that he needed my compliance. He needed to know I wasn't going anywhere.

I let out a whimper as his fingers glided over my hipbone and through my dark curls to dip between my legs. The whole time, his thick cock was right there, close enough to touch, so hard it was almost tight to his flat stomach.

"Fuck, you're wet, Emily."

I was. So fucking wet. I had no words to answer, so I spread my legs a little wider, tilting my hips to rub my clit over his fingers. A sweet charge of pleasure flashed through me.

"I had plans for you," he said. "Things I want to do to you. But they're going to have to wait. For now, I have to fuck you."

I'd never imagined hearing a man talk about fucking me would make me so hot. With anyone else, it probably wouldn't have, but there was something about hearing Tate say he had to fuck me that was almost as good as the real thing. Almost.

"Now, Tate. Please." It was all I could say. He took me over, pinning me down with his long body, sliding his hand around the back of my thigh to pull my knee up, spreading me wide for his cock. At the feel of him pressing into me, I whimpered. He was still too big, and I was too tight, but the pain was an erotic contrast to the thick hum of pleasure as Tate's body became a part of mine. He took me in shallow thrusts, easing his way in. By the time he filled me to the hilt, I was writhing beneath him.

One of his hands wrapped my wrists, still tangled in my bra, pinning them over my head. His mouth dropped to nip at my breasts. It was too much—the pressure between my legs, the raw flare of pleasure when his cock filled me, the dragging pull of bliss when he withdrew, the sharp little bites and slow sucks on my nipples. I was drowning in it, drowning in Tate, and all I could do was wrap my legs around him and hold on for the ride.

I heard myself breathing out his name, "Tate, Tate, Tate," over and over, utterly lost as every part of my body tumbled into orgasm, my pussy pulsing around his cock so hard I saw stars. He followed me, dropping his head to my neck, his mouth hot on my skin as he gasped out his release.

I couldn't move afterward. Neither could Tate. We lay there, panting for breath, one of his hands still holding my wrists over my head. Eventually, he untangled my bra and tossed it to the floor. He was gone less than a minute to deal with the condom, then slid back into the bed, pulling me into him. I rested my head on his shoulder, relaxing into Tate, trailing my fingers over the light speckle of hair on his chest.

"Was that too weird for you?" Tate asked.

"It was perfect," I said, not sure what he meant. Nothing he did was weird, especially the way he fucked me. "What part?"

"The hands. Your bra." He trailed his fingers over my wrist, lifting one to study the faint red marks—more a flush on my skin than anything that would bruise. I wasn't worried about it. I smiled into his warm skin at the memory of him holding my wrists down while he'd moved inside me.

"Not weird. I wondered what that would be like."

"And?"

"It was hot," I murmured. "Maybe next time, I'll hold you down."

"Would you like that?" Tate asked, his arm curling around my back to stroke the side of my breast.

"Mmm. I've done a lot of reading," I admitted. "I have a

lot of ideas, but I don't know what I'm doing yet. I think I need to practice on you."

"You can practice on me all you want, baby, as long as I'm the only one you practice with."

"Always," I said, suddenly serious. I rose onto my elbows so I could meet his eyes. "Always, Tate. Only you."

His lips curved in a smile, and he lifted one hand to draw me down for a kiss. His lips against mine, he vowed, "Always, Emily. Only you."

As promises went, it was everything I could have wished for. I knew life wouldn't always be easy with Tate, but I could handle it. I would make sure of it. Tate Winters was worth the risk, and he always would be.

Do you want Jacob & Abigail's story?
Keep reading for a sneak peek of
The Billionaire's Pet

SNEAK PEAK: THE BILLIONAIRE'S PET

CHAPTER ONE
Abigail

I sat on the plush leather sofa and stared at the thick wool carpet, trying not to count the scuffs on my shoes. John would have been so disappointed. The soft leather of my beige sling-backs was marked from walking through the wet grass before sunrise and my hair hung limp against my damp skin. John loved for me to look nice, always bragged that he had the prettiest wife in town. But John was gone and I was doing the best I could. Lately, my best had not included polishing my shoes.

This morning, my best had included a pre-dawn trek through the field behind the house I'd shared with John, a half mile hike through the woods separating the house from my cousin-in-law's small cabin, then a clandestine ride to the bus station two towns east. I hoped no one found out that Tina had helped me get to Atlanta. If I'd had another way, I'd never have put her at risk. But I'd had to reach Jacob Winters. He was the only one who could help me. I'd called his office from the bus station, arguing and pleading with the receptionist, then his assistant, to tell him I was on the line. After ten humiliating minutes, Jacob had clicked on, verified I was me, and told me he could fit me in at eleven for fifteen minutes. I'd spent the time in between lurking in a bookstore, knowing that the people already be looking for me would never think to look in a bookstore.

Jacob's office wasn't what I'd expected. I don't know where I got the image in my head, but I'd pictured it as slick and modern, filled with sleek black leather and chrome, his assistant as a svelte blond Valkerie. The couch was leather. I'd gotten that part right. But instead of cold black, it was a deep espresso, punctuated with dull brass tacks. The rug was an oriental design, the furniture not sharp and shiny, but antique, polished wood. And the woman at the desk, guarding the door to his office with disapproving eyes, was older than my mother, with a neat, chin length bob of grey hair that was heartbreakingly familiar.

An ugly irony that his assistant reminded me of my mother. The reason I was here. The reason I'd made almost every one of the disastrous mistakes I'd made in the last five years. If Anne Louise Wainright had any idea I was sitting in Jacob Winters's office, prepared to make him an offer I hoped he wouldn't refuse, she'd have passed out from the shock. Ladies did not consort with men not their husband. I'd been raised to be a lady, first, last, and always. It was why John had married me. But my mother no longer recognized me and my husband was dead. I'd made more than my share of bad decisions since my father had died and my mother had fallen ill. This would likely be one more. I was prepared to live with that. If Jacob could give me what I needed, I could find a way to live with anything.

A tone sounded at the assistant's desk. She pressed a

button, then murmured something I couldn't hear. My stomach clenched. I still had time to change my mind. I could stand up, make some flimsy excuse and be out on the city streets in no more than a few minutes. But what then? I couldn't go home. When Big John discovered me gone this morning he would have been furious. I didn't want to imagine what he would do to me if I came crawling back. His first proposal had been so appalling, my imagination recoiled from trying to picture what my father-in-law would consider an appropriate punishment for my defiance. If Jacob turned me away, I would lose everything. Not just my home and my mother, but my life as well.

"Miss Jordan?" The assistant stood in front of me, waiting with expressionless patience. The tension in my stomach congealed into a frozen ball of fear. I stood, wobbling only a little on my narrow heels. They were the sexiest pair I owned, bought in the early days of my marriage as a gift from John. They pinched my toes, were the worst shoes to wear when I'd spent a good part of my morning walking, but paired with my cream linen shift they made my legs look a mile long. I needed every advantage I could get. I tugged at the hem of my dress, smoothing the fabric as I followed the assistant to Jacob's door. I caught a whiff of her hairspray tangled with a perfume that smelled of roses and baby powder. She seemed too normal to be working for a man as magnetic as Jacob.

The assistant turned the brass handle and the door swung open on silent hinges. With a gesture, she indicated I should enter, then closed the door behind me. The click of the handle sent my heart thudding. No turning back now. All I could do was hope Jacob didn't throw me out when he heard what I had to say.

He walked toward me, his hand extended, a distant,

vaguely curious expression in his arresting silver eyes. Not a good sign. The way he looked at me was most of the reason I was here. That and the fact that he was the only man I could think of with the power to untangle my troubles.

The power was the 'how', but the way he'd looked at me was the 'why'. Or I'd hoped it would be. I hadn't met Jacob many times in the five years I'd been married to John. Only a handful of encounters, but each time I'd come away shaken. He was always controlled, gracious, reserved. Except when I caught him watching me on the sly. Then, his cool silver eyes had burned. With desire and intention. Jacob Winters wanted me. Not enough to risk his business with my in-laws, or maybe he'd known I'd never have cheated on John. Our marriage was so far from perfect it had devolved into a nightmare, but I still owed John too much to think about cheating. He hadn't deserved that kind of betrayal.

Steeling myself, I raised my hand to take Jacob's. His fingers were firm around mine, sending a shiver down my spine. I did my best to pretend confidence as I smiled up at him. He smiled back, his eyes warming a shade. A lock of thick, dark hair fell over his forehead, softening his sculpted face. Jacob Winters had the kind of looks that stopped a room. I'd seen it happen, at a cocktail party when John and I had been early and Jacob had been uncharacteristically late. He'd walked in and conversation had literally stopped, all eyes on Jacob handing off his coat as he brushed raindrops from his black hair.

He was taller than most men, at least a few inches over six feet. Broad shoulders, narrow torso, muscled but lean, and every woman who caught sight of him knew that without his trademark grey suits, he'd look even better. Smug gossip from the women who'd been there affirmed that as hot as he was when dressed, a naked Jacob Winters would ruin you for all other man. Hard to tell how much of that was bragging from women who wanted everyone to know they'd captured his elusive attention, even if it was only for a short time. I'd always thought they were under-stating his appeal. I never would have cheated on my husband, but if Jacob had asked, I would have been painfully tempted.

"Thank you for seeing me," I said, following Jacob deeper into his office. The space was divided into two sections, a sitting area with a couch, love seat and coffee table in the same style as the front room. Further into the long room was a huge desk of warm, caramel toned wood. A dark leather desk chair sat on the far side, two smaller leather armchairs opposite. To my surprise, Jacob led me to the desk. I'd thought, as the widow of a former business associate, he'd treat this more like a social visit. Wrong. There was no bullshitting Jacob that this was a social call. He'd sent flowers when John died. The niceties had been covered. The last minute call this morning, my insistence that I had to see him today, all told him this was business. So, the desk.

I took a seat in one of the arm chairs, crossed my legs and pasted a polite smile on my face. The training of my marriage. Don't show anything but what they want to see. Hide the panic. Hide the desperation. Slow, even breaths. Hands lightly clasped in my lap. I was the picture of calm elegance. Always.

"What's wrong?" Jacob asked, his sharp eyes pulling apart my facade. The instinctive protest that nothing was wrong jumped to my lips. I beat it back. Ridiculous to say nothing was wrong when everything was wrong.

"I'm in some trouble." I sat up straighter, tugging on the

hem of my dress. It was just a hair shorter than it should be, making it an alluring combination of classy and sexy. I'd worn it hoping it would sway Jacob in my favor. Now that I was sitting here in front of him, the amount of leg the cream linen exposed made me feel more vulnerable than confident.

"Do you know why I married John?" I asked, deciding to get straight to the point. It was a long story and he'd only given me fifteen minutes. Jacob sat back in his chair and shook his head.

"I'd always wondered. You never seemed like a good fit to me."

It was funny that Jacob would say that. Everyone else seemed to think we were the perfect fit. Me the sweet, spoiled banker's daughter and John the son of one of our small town's most powerful men. His family hadn't exactly been above board, but John was supposed to change all that. Marriage to me had cemented the image that his family was moving in more legitimate directions. Shortly after our wedding, he'd been invited to join the country club. In the beginning I'd taken over for my mother as a lady who lunched. No one had seen beneath the surface, because we hadn't let them.

"No," I said. "We really weren't." Taking a breath, I prepared for the confession I had to make. Five years later and I was still ashamed of what I'd done. "When I was sixteen, my mother began to develop early onset Altzheimers. By the time I graduated high-school she needed round-the-clock care. The summer after my sopho-more year in college, my father had a fatal heart attack."

"I'm sorry." Jacob leaned forward, compassion warming his demeanor. "That must have been very difficult for you at such a young age." I let out a bitter laugh, the harsh, short sound completely unlike the careful image I'd cultivated over the past few years.

"It would have been easier if I hadn't discovered that my father had lost everything he owned. The only miracle was that he'd kept everything at the bank clean. I don't know what I would have done if I'd had to pay them restitution."

"So you had nothing?"

"Nothing. The house, cars, artwork, my mother's jewelry. My grandmother's engagements rings. It was all sold. If it had just been me, I could have handled it."

"Your mother," he said. "I take it there wasn't any insurance to cover her care?"

"No. My father had her in an excellent facility by that time, but it was too expensive for me to handle on my own. And I wasn't qualified for the kind of job that could cover the bills and pay my rent. If I'd brought her home with me, I couldn't have gone out to work. I was trapped. And terrified."

"Let me guess, John walked in with the solution?"

I should have known Jacob would grasp the situation with a minimum of explanation. He might have lived and worked in the city an hour from our small country town, but he made it his business to know everything about the people he did business with. And he knew all he needed to know about the Jordan family. Far more than I had when I'd married John.

I'd grown up the sheltered, indulged daughter of our town's two leading citizens. I wasn't one of those privileged little snots that looked down on the rest of the world for not having the newest cars and clothes. My mother had, along with lunching at the country club, spent much of her time volunteering in our community. She'd taken me with her to food drives and literacy clinics, always wanting to make sure I understood how fortunate I was, and in my good fortune to remember to take care of those with less. While she'd managed to instill a sense of humility in me, my upbringing had not prepared me for the various ways life could turn ugly.

I knew about John's family. His father, Big John, was spoken of with respect and awe. Not the same kind of respect people had used when they'd spoken of my father. This was tinged with fear and a vague threat. I was never quite clear on what Big John did, or didn't do, to earn this type of regard. As far as I knew, he owned a plumbing supply company on the edge of town. When I asked, my father had told me it wasn't anything I needed to know. By the time I was in high school, I had the idea that some of Big John's enterprises weren't quite legal. But I hadn't understood what that meant. Not really. Not until it was too late.

"Yes." I straightened in the chair, as if correcting my posture could pull the shreds of my dignity together. "He offered to marry me. He was just back from college, ready to settle down and he said he'd always had his eye on me. He said that if we got married, he'd take over my mother's care. I didn't know what else to do."

"Like a lamb moving in with the wolves," Jacob commented, a wry smile on his face. "You had no idea what you were marrying into, did you?"

"None." I looked away from those knowing silver eyes, afraid I'd see pity. "It was the wrong thing to do. I know that. I told him I didn't love him. And I did my best to be a good wife. "

"You played the role he married you to play. Even when you knew what he was."

"Yes." I nodded. I'd married a man for his money. A man I liked, but would never love. The more I grew to know him, the less I even liked him. But I did my best to be what he wanted, always aware that he held my mother's life in his hands. She was far too fragile to leave the facility and only John's continued goodwill kept her safe and cared for.

"So why are you here?" Jacob leaned back in his chair, hands folded, resting on his chest. His eyes flicked to the clock on the wall. Time was ticking away, and I wasn't doing a very good job of getting to the point.

"Big John moved into the house a few days ago. He said that, with John gone, my debt was transferred to him. And if I wanted to see my mother taken care of, I'd do as he said."

"And what, exactly, did he say he wanted you to do? Sleep with him?" One dark, elegant eyebrow raised as if to ask if that was all it took to scare me off.

"Sleeping with him and keeping his house was just the beginning," I said. "He and John fought a lot at the end. One of the things they were fighting about was me. Big John felt that I was too big a drain on their resources. That I needed to earn my keep. He wanted to trade me out to some of their associates. John refused."

"You're kidding." Jacob's face darkened, his eyes shading from silver to a dark, forbidding gray.

"I wish I was."

"What did he say when you told him you wouldn't do it?"

"He said he had chains and drugs that would keep me in line. I acted like I'd go along, said I knew I owed him, but I had my period. Then I snuck out in the middle of the night." I fell silent, waiting. Jacob watched me, not speaking, for several endless minutes. Every muscle in my body was tight, tense to the point of pain. Jacob was my only chance. I had no money, no friends I'd risk to Big John's fury. Nowhere to go. Finally, he spoke.

"What do you expect me to do?"

This was the sticking point. The truth was, I didn't know. I wasn't asking for a job. After four years of marriage to John, I still had no marketable skills. All I had was my willingness to do anything to protect my mother.

"I can't take my mother out of the facility she's in. I can't afford to pay the fees. And I'm not sure, even if I turned my back on my mother, that I can stay clear of Big John. I need help with all of it." Jacob remained silent, studying me. I swallowed. It was against my temperament to push, but I didn't have a choice.

"I know it's a lot to ask. Too much. But I'll do anything." I stared him in the eye, daring him to doubt my commitment.

"Anything is a dangerous promise." Jacob tilted his head to the side. It should have been endearing. Instead it made him look like a predator studying his prey. Me. I swallowed before I spoke, my throat thick with nerves.

"Before I left, Big John said he was going to shoot me up with heroin and chain me to a bed while a gang of bikers rapes me. I'll do anything that stops short of drugs and rape." More silence. Then Jacob picked up the phone on his desk.

"Rachel, reschedule my 11:15." He hung up the phone and studied me another long minute before he spoke. "I want you. I wanted you the first minute I saw you. You know that. It's why you came to me."

"I—" I stopped speaking. Without knowing where he was going, I didn't want to dig myself a hole. I fell silent, waiting to hear what he would say.

"I have a circumstance I find difficult to handle, Abigail. Over the years I've tried various methods of dealing with it, and none have met with success. I've been thinking it's time to try something new. And you're going to be my something new."

My mind raced. Jacob's lips had curved into a smile at the word 'new'. His top lip was severe, the bottom lushly full. Together, they drew the eye. Especially in a half smile with a hint of mischief. His words, the smile, all sounded like he was going to help me. Now I just had to see what being his 'something new' would entail. Unable to force my mouth to move, I lifted my chin, inviting him to continue.

"I like sex," he said. "I like a lot of sex. A like variety. Kink. You've probably never heard of half of the things I've thought about doing to you. What I don't like is inconvenience." Jacob leaned forward, his eyes locked to mine, elbows resting on the polished wood of his desk.

"Relationships are inconvenient. They involve compromise, accommodation, and time. I don't have the patience for the first two and enough of the last. I don't want to get to know a women. I'm not interested in intimacy outside of sex. What I want is to fuck when I want to fuck. And I want to fuck a woman I'm attracted to who will let me do anything I want to her."

"Will you hurt me?" My voice was high and tight. I don't know what I was expecting, but this matter of fact, efficient speech wasn't it. It was, however, far less scary then Big John's proposal.

"Yes," he answered. My stomach pitched. "But I won't damage you. And the kind of hurt I'm talking about? You'll like it."

"So how does it work?"

"You move in with me. You don't leave the house. Ever. You do nothing without my permission. I'm not looking for a woman, I'm looking for a pet. An obedient, available pet. Can you do that?"

I stared, not sure I could answer. I'd walked in prepared to trade my body for my mother's safety. It wasn't honorable, but it was the only thing of value I had to offer. But this, his dehumanizing description of what he wanted from me, had shocked the speech from my brain. Lips and tongue frozen, I forced myself to nod. I couldn't afford for Jacob to think twice. No matter how terrifying this sounded, I couldn't run away. He stood, pushed back his chair, and rounded his wide desk. Standing in front of me, still seated in the leather armchair, he rested his hands on his hips and said,

"I think, before we go any further, I need a sample."

I stared up at him in dumb confusion. If my brain had been working, I'd have known exactly what he meant. Since I was slow, he clarified.

"Suck my cock."

ALSO BY IVY LAYNE

Don't Miss Out on New Releases, Exclusive Giveaways, and More!!

Join Ivy's Readers Group @ ivylayne.com/readers

THE HEARTS OF SAWYERS BEND

Stolen Heart

Sweet Heart

Scheming Heart

THE UNTANGLED SERIES

Unraveled

Undone

Uncovered

THE WINTERS SAGA

The Billionaire's Secret Heart (Novella)

The Billionaire's Secret Love (Novella)

The Billionaire's Pet

The Billionaire's Promise

The Rebel Billionaire

The Billionaire's Secret Kiss (Novella)

The Billionaire's Angel

Engaging the Billionaire

Compromising the Billionaire

The Counterfeit Billionaire

THE BILLIONAIRE CLUB

The Wedding Rescue

The Courtship Maneuver

The Temptation Trap

ABOUT IVY LAYNE

Ivy Layne has had her nose stuck in a book since she first learned to decipher the English language. Sometime in her early teens, she stumbled across her first Romance, and the die was cast. Though she pretended to pay attention to her creative writing professors, she dreamed of writing steamy romance instead of literary fiction. These days, she's neck deep in alpha heroes and the smart, sexy women who love them.

Married to her very own alpha hero (who rubs her back after a long day of typing, but also leaves his socks on the floor). Ivy lives in the mountains of North Carolina where she and her other half are having a blast raising two energetic little boys. Aside from her family, Ivy's greatest loves are coffee and chocolate, preferably together.

VISIT IVY
Facebook.com/AuthorIvyLayne
Instagram.com/authorivylayne/
www.ivylayne.com
books@ivylayne.com

Made in the USA
Monee, IL
01 November 2024

69118178R00075